William Hawley Smith

Walks Abroad and Talks about Them

William Hawley Smith

Walks Abroad and Talks about Them

ISBN/EAN: 9783337417666

Printed in Europe, USA, Canada, Australia, Japan

Cover: Foto ©Andreas Hilbeck / pixelio.de

More available books at **www.hansebooks.com**

WALKS ABROAD

AND

TALKS ABOUT THEM

BY

WILLIAM HAWLEY SMITH

AUTHOR OF

"THE EVOLUTION OF DODD"

———

1891

EDUCATIONAL PRESS ASSOCIATION

PEORIA, ILLINOIS

PRESS OF
J. W. FRANKS & SONS
PEORIA, ILL.

" I tramp a perpetual journey, and I ask you to come walk
    with me.
" And each man and woman of you I lead upon a knoll,
" My right hand pointing to landscapes of continents and the
    public road.
" Not I, not any one else, can travel that road for you.
" You must travel it yourself!
" So, shoulder your bundle, dear friend, and I will mine, and
    let us hasten forth.
" If you tire, give me both burdens, and rest your hand on my
    arm.
" And in due time you shall repay the same service to me.
" For, after we start, we shall never lie by again!   So,
" Come on! whoever you are, and let us travel together!
" Traveling with me, you shall find what never tires.
" The earth never tires!
" The earth is rude, silent, incomprehensible at first;
" Nature is rude and incomprehensible at first:
" But be not discouraged. Keep on. There are divine things
    there, well enveloped.
" There are divine things there more beautiful than words can
    tell!
" Come on! We must not stop here!
" However sweet these laid-up stores, however convenient this
    dwelling, we cannot remain here.
" However sheltered this port and however calm these waters,
    we must not anchor here.
" However welcome the hospitality that surrounds us, we are
    permitted to receive it but a little while.
" Come on! Yet take warning!

"*He traveling with me needs the best blood, thews, endurance.*

"*None may come to the trial till he or she bring courage and health.*

"*Come not here if you have already spent the best of yourself.*

"*Only those may come who come in sweet and determined bodies.*

"*Come on! after the Great Companions, and to belong with them!*

"*They, too, are on the road — they are the swift and majestic men — they are the greatest and grandest women!*

"*Come on! to that which is endless as it was beginningless.*

"*To undergo much, tramp of days, rest of nights;*

"*To see nothing, anywhere, but that you may reach it and pass it;*

"*To conceive of no time, however distant, but that you may reach it and pass it;*

"*To look up or down no road but it stretches and waits for you — however long, it stretches and waits for you!*

"*Whoever you are, come forth! or man or woman, come forth!*

"*You must not stay sleeping and dallying there in the house, though you built it, or though it was built for you.*

"*Come on! the road is before us!*

"*It is safe — I have tried it — my own feet have tried it well.*

"*Come on!*

"*Comrade, I give you my hand!*

"*I give you my love, more precious than money;*

"*I give you myself, before all preaching or law;*

"*Will you give me yourself? Will you come and travel with me;*

"*Shall we stick by each other just as long as we live?*"

INDEX.

WALKS ABROAD.

THE OUTSET.

In that far distant era when our "entering class" stood up around Mary Montague's knees and learned our letters in the orthodox fashion of taking the alphabet "in course," as everybody was expected to take everything in those days, I remember that that motherly old maid of a Yankee schoolmarm gave us some "supplementary work," as it would be called now, in the shape of little verses that we learned and recited in concert, our arms entwined around each other, and the whole little charmed circle swaying and weaving, back and forth, in even time, as we said the lines over in a sing-song way. And among these verses, thus learned and recited, there was one that began :

> "Whene're I take my *walks abroad*,
> How many ——s I see."

I have forgotten just what the word was that fitted in where I have left a blank ; nor do I know why my memory should have failed to hold the particular monosyllable that evidently belongs in there, while clinging fast to all the rest of the lines ; but after nearly fifty years' acquaintance with this mental furniture of mine, I have quit trying to account for all its peculiarities—omissions, commissions and what not.

There was some word of one syllable that went there, and, as I look at it now, I find that it does not make so very much difference what it was, for any one of a hundred will do just as well as the one the original rhymer used.

And, perhaps, after all, it is fully as well to let the blank stand, and permit each reader to fill it in "as occasion requires or opportunity offers," as our pastor says in prayer meeting.

And so I am not going to worry my head about the original word, nor shall I care a straw if any delver after "primary forms" should hunt out this old fossil and send me the particular chip which is lacking in the specimen I have shown above ; for, put any *one* word in this niche and it narrows the same down to the particular thing which that one word stands for, and this leaves the lines far less true to the reality than they are with my blank holding up the heavy end of the iambus in this particular line. So I leave it as it is, merely remarking that there are a good many other things in this old world that are similar to this. It does not pay to try to put them into their original forms, for they are better to us as we have them. Doubtless, it will not do to carry this argument too far ; but, run to a reasonable length, it works well and yields most blessed results.

And so, as I was about to remark, "When e're i take my walks abroad," — as I do every day and sometimes several times a day, — I see more things than any *one* word can stand for ; and when a man undertakes to put words in my mouth which shall tell what I am doing, I want those words to tell the whole story, or else to stand back and give me a chance to speak for myself. Or, perhaps, we can compromise the matter ; the rhymer may tell all of my story he can and I will do the rest. I will take these lines, just as I have quoted them, reserving only the blank for myself, to fill in as I choose ; and, just as the magic lantern man reserves for himself a little blank slot in his instrument into which he can slip any "slide" that he can get hold of, and always with a varied effect, so I will keep this blank open, and into it I will slip, from time to time, the things I see "whenc're I take my walks abroad."

A HUNTER'S PHILOSOPHY.

I went out hunting a few days ago — took a walk abroad among sedge-grass and cockle-burs, down along the river bottom, where cranes are wont to congregate and croak, where mud-hens multiply and chuckle to each other in the secret places of swamp and fen, and where, occasionally — very occasionally — a duck disports itself, a half a mile or so from shore, out of range of any weapon, unless it be a howitzer or Gatling-gun.

But we went hunting, just the same ; walked and talked as of yore, and did several things besides, things which this chronicle has no particular business with, and which for that reason will be omitted from this truthful tale.

There was one novelty about our trip this season ; we all took rifles instead of shotguns. The matter was settled at a meeting of the club, a month or so ago. At this meeting some discussion arose about skill in marksman-ship, and a very eloquent member made a telling speech about rifle-shooting as contra-distinguished from shotgun ditto.

The point he made was that the marksman who could bag game as the result of a single bullet sent after each particular bird, by that very act proved himself an artist with a fowling-piece ; while the man who used a shotgun, which belches forth a thousand leaden pellets at each discharge, and these scattered over a wide area, could never tell whether he really was a good shot, or whether his awkwardness in shooting all ways at once should be credited with his success as a sportsman.

The talk on the subject ran high for a while ; and, finally, to settle the matter for one year, at least, it was agreed that we should all take rifles on our annual outing this season.

So we all took rifles.

My own gun was of the most recent make, manufactured in the East, and by a firm which has a most excellent and enviable reputation for making the best goods of the kind to be had in this or any other market. The maker's name was stamped upon the barrel as a guarantee that the article was genuine.

And it was really a good gun. I think it was all it was ever recommended to be, and I have no word of fault to find with it as a gun ; nevertheless, I shot with it for **two** days and never touched a feather !

Of course this was unpleasant ; for, formerly, on a shotgun basis, I had always managed to bring in about an average bagful of game ; and now to come in empty-handed, two days in succession, was little less than disgrace. It seemed to establish the truth of my eloquent friend's theory that my record as a sportsman depended upon my promiscuous, rather than upon my definite and direct shooting — a conclusion which was **by** no means flattering to my self-esteem, to say nothing of my vanity. But the third day I set out as before, and, as good luck would have it, I came upon a fine flock of ducks in a small pool, within easy range of a thick clump of brush which served me as a cover. The birds had not discovered my approach, and were disporting themselves with the utmost nonchalance as I made ready to shoot. I drew a bead on a large drake that sat perfectly still about fifty yards away, and fired !

If ever I was sure of game in my life it was just at the moment when I pulled the trigger of that gun. But the result was the same as before ; or, rather, worse, for this time the birds did not even do me the honor to fly. They only lifted their heads for a minute, as though a bit surprised, and then went to feeding again.

To say that I was disgusted is to but feebly express my emotions as I lay hidden in that clump of bushes, and for four successive times blazed away at those unconcerned and aggravating ducks, which now seemed to be growing accustomed to my fusilade, and rather to enjoy than to fear it. I blamed the gun and those who made it. I called myself names, and grew red in the face. I —

But just as I was making ready for the fifth shot, and had declared to myself that I would smash my gun into smithereens if I did not kill that time, I heard a slight noise on my left, and turning, I saw the burly form of an old river hunter lying full length in the bushes not ten feet from me. He had heard my firing, and I think out of sheer curiosity had crawled into my cover to see what it was all about.

He was a typical man ·of his class, rough, bearded, tanned to a copper color, and dressed in yellow jeans. He had never belonged to a gun club, and I doubt if he at all knew the meaning of " Extra Dry." I am quite sure he could not have passed a written examination on " Sportsmanship from an Esthetic Point of View," especially if

the professor in our club had had the privilege of preparing the questions; but the *denoument* showed that he
knew a thing or two, for all that.

I have said that I saw him, etc. Evidently he had
been in his present position for some time, and had witnessed my former endeavors and failures, for as soon as I
caught his eye he said, under his breath :

"*You d — n fool, lower your hind-sight ! Ha'nt you got
sense enough to see that you are shootin' over 'em every time !*"

I "lowered my hind-sight," and we had ducks for
supper out of my bag that night.

———

I was sitting on the platform at an educational gather-
ing, not long ago, and the professor in charge was dictating some very excellent words to the teachers there
assembled, reading from a book, a few words at a time,
the teachers writing as he read, thus :

"It should be the aim of education — to effect the
triune result — etc., etc."

There were about a hundred teachers writing, and
when the reader pronounced the word "triune," I think
at least ninety of the writers looked up for an instant and
scowled inquiringly, then dropped their eyes and hurried
on with their notations. The reader made no pause at
this demonstration — took no notice of it, in fact, but went
on dictating, a few words at a time, to the end of the somewhat long and stilted, not to say slightly high-flown sentence, his listeners writing as best they could.

The exercise was continued for about fifteen minutes,
and among the sentences dictated occurred the words,
"apperception," "conjunctivity," "curricula," "adumbration," and a few more of about the same size and
weight. And every time one of these words was shot into

that audience, so to speak, there was the same lifting of heads, inquiring elevation of eyebrows, scowl, and return to writing on the part of about nine out of every ten of those who were doing their best to set down what the reader of the book was saying.

When all was over, I asked the professor if he would call on some one who had been writing to read what he or she had written. He readily consented, and at once asked a very bright-looking girl, of about twenty, who sat just before him, to stand and read her notes. She blushed and looked down, hesitatingly, and finally said:

"I can't do it."

"Why not?" said the professor.

"I haven't got it all written down," replied the girl.

"Did I read too fast?" said the professor.

"No, I guess not," said the girl.

"Well, then, what's the matter?" said the professor.

The girl hesitated and blushed still deeper, while there was an anxious look on nearly every face in the room.

It was at this point that I begged for a word, and asked the young lady if she would read as far as she had written, be the same more or less. She was a brave girl (it takes genuine bravery, and a good deal of it, to do what I asked her to do, the circumstances being what they were) and so, with a resolute, not to say half desperate motion, she rose and read:

"It should be the aim of education to effect the——"

She stopped, and I said:

"Well?"

"I didn't understand the next word," she said.

"How many in the room *did* understand the next word, and have it written down?" I asked.

There was a pause; then some two or three hands went up promptly and perhaps half a dozen timidly, but the ninety held their peace.

"Will all who did *not* get the word written down please to stand?" I asked. "Come! It's no disgrace to say we don't know when we don't know," I added.

And then there was a sound as of a rushing mighty wind, and the ninety arose, *en masse*.

The professor looked puzzled. He was a clever gentleman, and a most thorough scholar, and he read exceptionally well, in a clear, full voice, pronouncing every word distinctly, and how it was that all these people had missed this word of two syllables was more than he could comprehend.

And then I said to a young man who stood in front: "What was the matter with the word that you did not get it?" And he replied: "I don't think I ever heard it before!" Whereupon, these words have been spoken, eighty-nine pairs of eyes, or thereabouts, looked into mine and said as plain as eyes can say anything, "That's just it!"

I confess that I was a good deal surprised at this generous and wholesale confession on the part of these teachers, for the word in question had hardly struck me as being so very unusual and the people before me were by no means dull or dumb. On the contrary, they were more than averagely bright Nevertheless, the great fact remained that the word "triune" was a stranger to their eyes and ears thus far!

Not to prolong the story, the professor took the cue and proceeded with a still further reading of the notes taken from his reading only to find "apperception," "conjunctivity," "curricula," "adumbration," and several more of similar sort among the things that were not.

At dinner, just before this exercise, I had told the

professor my hunting experience, narrated above, and after he had staggered along with this notes-reading for about ten minutes, and had found out what a thing of shreds and patches it was in reality, when compared with what he had expected it to be, he turned to me and said, under his breath.

"*It looks a good deal as though I had better lower my hind sight.*"

And I think he was right about it too.

The fact is, it is a common fault to shoot over:—

"Agitate the water, Michael," said a clergyman to an Irishman who was cleaning out his well.

"An' phat the divil is that?" said Mike.

"Stir it up," said the man at the windlass, and it was done!

I have a friend who is the most brilliant scholar of my acquaintance, but he delights in polysyllables, and his language is of the strictly classical sort. The maid-of-all-work in his kitchen is a Swede, who, while she is an excellent cook, speaks English only on the installment plan, with very limited installments at that. My friend tried to tell her something to do, the other day, and after several most eloquent efforts he gave up in despair. He hunted up his wife (a very sensible and plain spoken woman, she is), and told her that he "could not make that stupid girl understand." (He reads Greek, Latin, French, German and Italian.). The good woman listened to his tale of woe, and then went and told the girl what to do, using simple words that were easily understood. When she came back she remarked to her husband: "My dear, if you would be less Johnsonese you would be far more understandable."

And as he loves peace and quiet at home he at once proceeded to "lower his hind sight."

And there is that other acquaintance of mine, who told me that not long ago he sat down to write a lecture, and how he covered six full pages with a most brilliant introduction, all filled with "hyperbole, metaphor, mettonomy, prosodypeia, superbaton, cattychraysis, mettylipsis, and hustheron-protheron," as Father Tom has it. Having written so much, he took it down and read it to his wife. And *she, too*, is a most sensible woman. (These women, God bless them! How could we get on without them?) She heard him through, and then said, quietly: "Oh, Charles, come off the perch!"

And to his credit be it said, he did as he was told.

But I think it is in the school-room, more than anywhere else, that we "shoot over," and so ought to "lower the hind sights" of our pedagogical guns, as it were. Indeed I am certain that any teacher will be surprised, not to say appalled, if he or she will carefully watch the effect, or rather the *lack* of effect, that their words have upon pupils. The young people hear what we say, perhaps so far as the material ear is concerned, but they do not understand and we are to blame because they do not.

We talk of predicate-nominatives and substantive phrases to ten and twelve-year-olds, in the grammar class, and these long-range missiles fly yards and yards over and beyond the game they are aimed at! We fire involution and permutation into droves of eighth-graders. They "duck their heads" for a minute, and then go on chewing gum just as though nothing had happened, careless alike of ourselves and of the noises we make.

And this is the really pitiful, not to say tragic, thing about it all. *Our young people get into the habit of listening to words that make no impression upon them,* and the result is that they very soon get careless, especially upon all educational matters. Or, perhaps I should say they get discouraged.

No one likes to be continually listening to what he does not understand, and if long compelled to do so, he will either be bored beyond endurance, or involuntarily and unwittingly get a poor opinion of his ability to understand and comprehend what it is supposed he ought to learn about.

And if a pupil gets in the way of thinking that he is not going to understand, the chances are many to one that he will not understand; and when he has reached that point, the limit of educational growth, in that direction, is close at hand.

The true test of really great things is their simplicity. They are so easily understood by everybody. In that wonderful art gallery at the World's Fair, it was the simple pictures that drew the crowds, the ones that all understood, and crowded upon each other to look at. "Breaking Family Ties," "Preparing for the Wedding," "The Alarm," "The Reply," and a thousand more that could be named—these are the great works of art, and they are simple and as easily understood as they are incomparable as artistic productions.

And the same is true in other lines of art. It is now e.ght years since Mr. Denman Thompson brought out that simplest of all dramas, "The Old Homestead," but he is still playing it to crowded and ever delighted audiences. "Uncle Tom's Cabin" is simplicity itself in plot, execution, and language, but a world has read it, with weeping eyes, and knows the story by heart.

It is further recorded of the Master of us all that "the common people heard him gladly."

How are you shooting beloved?

THROUGH MEMORY'S WAYS.

While I was waiting my turn at the bank, the other day, I overheard the following conversation between the cashier and a customer who stood the third man ahead of me, his nose almost against the little brass-grated window, as he spoke:

Customer—"Do you remember the number of that draft on Chicago which you gave me one day last week?"

Cashier —"No, sir, I don't. It is a rule of this bank to *remember nothing*. But if you can tell me the date on which you got the draft, I can readily find the number for you."

Whereupon, the date being given by the customer aforesaid, it was the work of but an instant for the cashier to turn to the *record of drafts* issued on that day, and there find the desired information.

Shortly afterwards I passed a leading merchant of the city in conversation with a gentleman with whom he evidently had the most amicable of business relations, and this is what I heard him say, as I went along:

"No, don't ask me to *remember* your order, but go down to the store and leave a memorandum of what you want, and then you are sure to get it. But if I should try to remember it for you, the chances are a hundred to one that you wouldn't see the goods for six months."

And when I went to the sash factory, and ordered a sash made to fit our north cellar window (we are going to have double sash in that window this winter, sure. We have *thought* for the last five years that we would fix it that way, but, somehow, have always *forgotten* it till now.

But wife made a *memorandum* about it, one day last week, and put the same where I couldn't help seeing it, and so the sash is ordered.) I say, when I told the sash man what I wanted, he said, "Make a memorandum, please, of just the size you want, and there will be no mistake in filling your order."

And so it was that, when I went to the tailor for a suit of clothes, he measured me up one side and down the other, as smart as you please, calling out the inches and fractions of an inch, of each measurement in a good round tone, while his clerk wrote all these numbers down in a book, where they are, even unto this day, showing just what manner of man I am, so far as size and shape are concerned, beyond all question or cavil.

We lost some freight, some time since, and asked the railroad company to look it up for us. So they sent out a "tracer" for the goods—that is, a letter, that should follow along the same route that the goods were supposed to have traveled. This letter went, first, to the freight office from which the goods were originally shipped. The agent there referred to his *record* regarding this particular package of merchandise. He found that he had received it from the transfer company, and had billed it out, on a certain train, to a certain station where it was to be transferred to another line of road. That cleared his skirts. Then he wrote a letter to the agent at the station where the package was to have been transferred, described the goods, told what train they were shipped on, and asked him to show up what he knew about them. This agent referred to his *record*, found out what disposition he had made of the package, and so on; till, finally, the goods were found and laid down at their proper destination.

I saw a drug clerk fill out a prescription, not long ago

and I noticed that he followed the doctor's *written direc-tions*, explicitly; and when he had the mixture com-pounded, he filed the original prescription, which was numbered to correspond with the label on the bottle, on a hook, where if could be referred to, years hence, if need be.

And when I went to my dentist with a tooth which was giving me trouble, and which I assured him he had filled some years before, he astonished me by turning to a *record* of the work he had done for me for the past ten years, and, to use the vernacular, this particular tooth "wasn't in it" at all. The simple truth was that I was mistaken, and had *forgotten* that it was a dentist a thou-sand miles from here who filled the molar that was now giving offense.

Once I was in the office of the *Youth's Companion* and the manager kindly showed me how they handle their voluminous mail (thousands of letters a day), with so much ease and accuracy. Thus, the letters are all opened by a clerk whose particular business is to do just this work. He makes a hasty glance at the contents of each letter, and long practice has enabled him to determine unerringly, and with great despatch, the proper depart-ment to which each one should be referred. This done, he puts his stamp upon the document, showing that it has been through his hands and referred, and deposits it in some one of several baskets that are ranged about him, each basket holding letters for a separate department. The contents of these baskets are carried to their several de-partments and there disposed of by the various clerks in those departments. Every clerk who has anything whatever to do with any letter that comes into his or her hands *puts his mark and memorandum* on the same, for future reference, if such should ever be required.

When all is done, the letter is filed where it can readily be referred to, and on its blank spaces there is a *written record* of every one's hands it has passed through, and just what each one has done. If there is ever any trouble, if a mistake has been made, anywhere, it is an easy matter to trace the whole business up, and find out just who it was that made the error, and what the error was that was made. All such errors are charged up to the clerks who make them, and on this record clerks are promoted or deposed. Those who make few mistakes go up; those who blunder go down—and out, if the same thing happens more than a fixed number of times.

Now what I started out to say was, that in all these instances that I have cited, there isn't as much *memory work*, all put together, as is given the average pupil in our public schools any half day in the year. In a word, in the business world it is a fundamental principle not to try to *remember* anything. And this means, I take it, that *experience has demonstrated the fact that the memory is such a treacherous faculty that it is not at all to be relied upon for exact data regarding the things that are past.*

And yet, to what infinite lengths of labor do our schools and colleges go to "develop the memory." The question I wish to raise is, is the game worth the candle? Is this faculty of the human mind of enough importance to have three-fourths of all the time spent in school devoted to its "development"? And, more than all, does the titanic strain that is put upon the memory by all our school courses—does this tend to strengthen that faculty; or, rather, does it not tend to deplete it? To a consideration of this question, "let facts be submitted to a candid world."

And to get such submission of facts, oh my dear

reader, all you have to do is to get inside of *yourself,* and take a memory-invoice of what stock of that sort *you* have on hand at this day and date. That will tell the story, so far as you are concerned; and to you, that is better than the testimony of ten thousand other folks. So get at it now, and see how it comes out in your case.

And, first, was the game worth the candle, so far as *you* are concerned? Did you get net results from burning the midnight oil, while you strove to *memorize* the area and population of each state in the union, to say nothing of the rivers, lakes, mountains, towns, cities, and what not; from getting lists of dates so that you could say them backwards or forwards or "skipping around;" from learning atomic weights and combining numbers so that you could say them without the book ; from getting all the grammar rules so that you could repeat them, every one, in order ; or from saying over punctuation rules, which you never did see any sense in, and never could apply — I say, out of all this monstrous mass of memory work that *you* did in school, have you ever got enough to pay you for all the time and trouble you went to, to get good enough marks out of it all to graduate on ? How is it ?

I have figured the thing through, in my own case, and have "got the answer." I won't ask you to memorize it, but I will write it down, right here, where you can refer to it any time you want to. And this it is : *It did not pay me.*

And I do not say this unadvisedly. Look at it in any way I may, the result is the same. If I say, " How much of this matter, that I strove so hard to memorize while a student in school, have I had occasion to use since I left school ?" I am appalled at the paucity of opportunities for the utilization of what I worked so diligently to get.

And if I ask, "How much of what I could then recite without the book do I still hold in my memory?" I am startled at the percentage of loss.

Why, I cannot now give the area or population of a single state in the Union, though I learned them all, thoroughly, twenty-five years ago. And as for historic dates, atomic weights, punctuation rules, and the whole line of similar things that I sat up, night after night, to learn, they are a blank to me now — an utter blank.

But what do I care for that? There is a cyclopedia over there on the shelf (I can almost reach it without getting out of my chair, as I write), and it holds all these things without an effort — keeps them ready and waiting for me, whenever I have occasion to use them. And so, if I want to know the area of New York, or the population of California, all I have to do is to turn to the page, and, there you are! Right, too. No guess-work. No "I think it is," or "as I remember it." Nothing of that sort, but good, honest figures, that time will not blot out or get mixed up.

And there is the chemistry over there, and here are the histories (oh, how easy it is for them to hold those dates, thousands of them; and what delight it is to me to go and find them, just right, when I want them). And the grammar and punctuation-book—though, to be honest, I never do refer to that. I learned to punctuate after I got out of school; in such an easy way, too, and wholly without that book. I was talking, one evening, with a friend, and he said: "The way to learn to punctuate is to punctuate." "But," I said, "I can't. I don't know how. I studied the art for six months, in school; but, somehow, I can't do anything at it." "Well," said he, "I will tell you how to learn to punctuate. Notice, carefully, how the articles you read in any good magazine, or metropolitan newspaper, are punctuated, and stop your reading every once in a while, and ask yourself why any given sentence is punctuated as it is, and you will be surprised to find how soon you will learn to punctuate well."

And I did as he told me, and I found it to be even as he had said. And I see no good reason why my teacher in punctuation could not have used a sensible method of this sort, and taught me punctuation so that I could punctuate, instead of spending the time trying to develope my memory by making me learn punctuation rules and exceptions — largely exceptions — that I didn't understand and never could apply! So, I never refer to the punctuation-book.

But I do refer to nearly all the other books in my library, as I have need. Occasionally I turn the pages of some old school book, for reference, but I am sure I could do it equally well now, even if I had not been forced to *memorize the whole volume* when a student.

No! to my mind our schools are all wrong in giving their pupils so much memory work, and I am certain that their so doing does not strengthen the memory nor cultivate the mind. On the other hand, I am convinced that it debilitates the mnemonic faculty and tends to stupify the intellect.

It is a well recognized principle in physiology that if you overtax an organ you thereby weaken it. We overburden the memories of our pupils, and thereby weaken that faculty in them. We give them such memory-loads to carry that they cannot stand up under them, and so they throw them off at the very first chance they can get. All they try to do is to hold on to the matter until they can pass an examination in it, and then they let it all slip; as, surely, they are obliged to do, to make room for a new load. And so it is that *they fall into the habit of forgetting* rather than *remembering* — an outcome which is the very reverse of what was promised — and paid for!

Just here I got to wondering how it happens that our schools have fallen into such abnormal ways of teaching, and here is what has come to me about it. I wonder if this predominance of memory-work in our schools is not a direct descendent from the methods used in the days *when there were no books!* In those times the only way in which the knowledge of one could be made available by another was for that other to *remember* it. The only way for the pupil to acquire the knowledge which the teacher had to impart was to commit it to memory, and the only way the teacher could know that his pupil had acquired what he had imparted was to test his memory about it.

And this is how "*exams.*" came into being. They were all right and proper in their time, and, as such, they took rank and place in an educational system. But when the era of *books* came, they became antiquated methods, and would long ago have been dropped, but for the persistence of habit. What a powerful force habit is!

Well, if these things are so (and I see no good reason to doubt them), it is perfectly clear that we ought to let up, greatly, on the memory work that is now doing in our schools.

"But," some one says, "didn't Edward Everett get so that he could read a newspaper through, and then fold it up and recite every word that it contained? and could not Prof. Watson recite a full table of logarithms, true to six places, without ever referring to a book? etc., and so on to the end of the chapter. Yes, verily, these men could do these things; and "Uncle Dick" Oglesby can, to this day, call by his first name every man in the one hundred and two counties in Illinois that he has ever been introduced to; and I know a man who can charm birds,

and nearly all other animals — make them do almost anything he wishes to have them do; and there is an old
hunter up the river who will shoot a duck on the wing,
nine times out of ten, and never bring his gun to his
shoulder — just hold it against his side, and, without
taking sight at all, blaze away and down his game every
time; and Bishop Whatley, as a boy of six, could work
mathematical problems, mentally, in a few minutes, that
it would take his father some hours to figure out, though
the old gentleman was himself apt at figures; and Blind
Tom can hear a piece of music once, and play it over
exactly; and John L. Sullivan can strike a blow with his
fist, that will fell an ox; and Jay Gould made a $100,000,-
000, because he had it in him to do just that.

But, forsooth, because these things are so it does not
follow that methods should be introduced into our public
schools whose purpose it should be to enable *every pupil*
to call by his first name every man he might ever be introduced to; or to tame birds, lions and all other wild fowl;
or to shoot without taking sight; or to mentally acquire
a product of twenty places; or to strike with the fist like
a sledge-hammer; or to make $100,000,000 out of nothing
but manipulation!

Now, the fact is that the miraculous *memory feats* of
Mr. Everett and Mr. Webster and Mr. Gladstone and all
of their kind, that have been held up for our emulation
and imitation, are phenomenal. These men did these
wonderful things because they were born with special gifts
in that line, and it is just as nonsensical to talk about
making every boy and girl in our schools work toward the
attainment of these achievements as it would be to try to
make them all develop heads of the size of Mr. Webster's,
or play like Blind Tom, or strike like Sullivan. And yet
this memory training is upheld because these memory

giants did these wonderful things. It is time this delusion was abandoned.

Because, the truth is that *memory is not such an important faculty of the mind that it should receive the great bulk of all the attention that is given to mental training in our schools.* And yet it does so receive, the country over, to-day. To be plain about it, this memory of ours, however drilled, is one of our most treacherous mental possessions. No business man ever relies on it in any matter where absolute accuracy is required. In our courts, the testimony of witnesses who mean to tell the truth and who do their best to do so, but who fail to tell things as they really occurred, because their memory has played them false, shows how unreliable this mental faculty is. Ask any lawyer or judge, and he will tell you all about it ; or, probably, you know well enough about it yourself. I do.

The other day I was on the witness-stand, and was asked if I had not, about three years before, received a certain letter from one of the parties to the suit. My impulse was to testify that I never received any such letter, or any letter whatever, from the person in question ; but, to make the matter sure, I said that I had no *recollection* of ever receiving any letter from the party ; but, I added, "if I ever did receive such a letter it would be on file in my office." When I came off the stand, the judge told me that I might go and look for that letter, since, if it were written, as claimed, it would be important evidence. I went and looked for it, *and found it*, with my own indorsement on it of having answered it myself in the regular course of business ! And yet I had no recollection whatever of the entire transaction.

And I know that my experience in this is not unique. You know it is "common," do you not ? And because it is so, because memory is such a tricky part of our mental furniture, I do not believe that it is wise to spend three-fourths of all the time in our schools in trying to "cram" it. We can use the time better in some other way. Don't you think so ?

P. S. – After I had this chapter written I read it to a teacher, a friend of mine, and he said : "You are fighting a man of straw. They don't teach now-a-days as they did when you went to school." I said nothing, but as in the next six days I had the opportunity of being in as many different towns, I took the liberty of dropping into a couple of schools in each town to see how they taught school *there.* Then I came home and copied out the paper, just as I had written it, only I underscored some words that I had not thought it necessary to emphasize when I wrote the first copy.

TO YOU

On looking over the printed edition of the foregoing chapter I find that I made a capital blunder in the manuscript for the same—an error that I want to rectify here as far as I can. The last sentence in the article proper—the one that comes just before the "P. S." is a question, and it reads, "Don't you think so?" That is the way I wrote it, and as a most natural consequence, that is the way it was printed. Nevertheless, as it stands, it does not begin to utter what I wanted it to say, nor express what I meant to put into it.

What I ought to have done was to have underscored the word "you" in my copy, so that the printed edition would have read "Don't *you* think so?" That would have put a point upon all that had gone before, and perhaps made it penetrate at least one or two *individual souls, personally*, pricking them up to veritable action in the premises; whereas, leaving the thing general, as I did, to apply to anybody or everybody (or more probably *nobody*) the whole force of all I had said stands a good chance of coming to nothing—going out into empty space, and vanishing into glittering generalities.

Because, you see, it is only as what is written or said strikes *you*, in especial, and takes hold of *you*, and leads *you* to action, that it is worth while writing or saying anything at all. I mean *really* worth while. Of course, one may write merely for the sake of making marks on paper, or talk merely for the sake of wagging one's tongue, or one may read merely to kill time; but none of these things are really *worth while*, according to my way of thinking. Who is it that says, "I do not write these things for a dollar, nor to fill in the time while I wait for a boat?" Aye, truly! Neither does any man or woman who has come to realize that life is really worth living!

And yet we are all so prone to let the things that would fain hit us hard, glance off, and be shivered into a million fragments of generalities, rather than suffer them to be focused to a needle-point fineness, and stick into our souls *individually*, and rankle there, piercing even to the dividing asunder of the joints and of the marrow, of the soul and of the body, if need be; goading us to action, whether we wish it or no; filling us with unrest until we *do* what the stern behest tells us we *ought* to do!

I remember an old deacon in the church into which I was born, who said one evening at church meeting, when the brethren were discussing the merits and demerits of a new minister they were about to "call," and some one intimated that his sermons were not practical—that this old worthy remarked that he did not know or care a fig whether the sermons were practical or not; that he didn't think he should know a practical sermon if he ever heard one; that he liked a sermon as he liked a meal of victuals—all he asked of it was that it should go in one ear and out the other, and be good while it was going.

He was a notorious old skinflint, one who would devour a widow's house with no more apparent feeling than as if he were killing a fly. Yet, he heard the Word, every Sunday; but there was no *personality* in it for him, and the messages of truth and grace that fell from the preacher's lips simply "went in at one ear and came out at the other," so far as he was concerned, and they were "good while they were going" because they only applied to somebody else.

I lost sight of the old fellow when I was a mere boy, and I do not know what finally became of him, but I have often thought what a rattling of dry bones there must have been in his case, if ever he came to a place where someone pointed a finger straight at him, and said, "Thou art the man," so that it stuck clear through him and came out on the other side.

And yet I would have no harsh word for this rigid old Puritan, for we are all more or less apt to be like him, in that we are very willing to let the great lessons of life *for us* go by, while we shy along on the other side of the road. Nevertheless, the things that count for any of us, and the only things that really count, are those that we take *personally* to ourselves, and that sink so deep into us that they move us this way or that, for good or for ill, as the case may be.

And so it is that I am anxious that what I write shall hit *you*, my dear reader, and move *you* to action, one way or the other. Not that I expect, or even hope that you will agree with me in all, or perhaps in any part, of what I say. I should be the veriest goose, not to say fool, to think such a result possible. And, indeed, for this I have no care whatever.

Of course, if what I have to say strikes you as true, and, so doing, stirs you up to action on the lines of what seems to *me* to be right, then I am indeed glad. But if, reading any words of mine, your soul says, "No, he is wrong there, and I *know* it, for I have worked the thing through on my own account, and I am as certain as I am that I am alive that he is in error"—if your soul says that to you, and you act accordingly, and rise up in the might of truth and demolish every word that I have ever written—why then, so long as you have *the truth* on your side, I thank you, from the bottom of my heart, for pointing out my error, and count you the dearest and most faithful friend I ever had.

But to have my words fall flat on *you*, to have to realize that, for *you*, they merely go in at one eye and out at the other, and are good while they are going, this is wormwood to me.

And so I wish I had written the question originally, "Don't *you* think so?"

All of which leads me to the reflection that no man or woman in all this world amounts to much till he or she comes to realize what an important part of creation they, each one, *personally*, are, viewed from their own *individual* standpoint. And this, not in any offensively egotistical way, but merely as a matter of fact that arises from the very nature of things, in that every living human being is an immortal soul, and as infinite as eternal!

And so it is that, *so far as* YOU *are concerned*, no matter who you are:

"*You* are he or she for whom the earth is solid and liquid.
"*You* are he or she for whom the sun and moon hang in the sky.
"Whoever you are, motion and reflection are especially for *you*.
3

" Whoever you are, the divine ship, this wondrous world ot ours, sails the divine sea especially for *you*.

" For none more than *you* are the present and the past.

" And for none more than *you* is immortality.

" Each man to himself, and each woman to herself, is the word of the past and present, and the word of immortality.

" No one can acquire for another—not one!

" No one can grow for another—not one!

" The song is to the singer, and comes back most to him.

" The teaching is to the teacher, and comes back most to him.

" The murder is to the murderer, and comes back most to him.

" The theft is to the thief, and comes back most to him.

" The love is to the lover, and comes back most to him.

" The gift is to the giver, and comes back most to him—it cannot fail.

" The oration is to the orator, and the acting to the actor and actress, not to the audience.

" And no man understands any greatness or goodness but his own, or the indications of his own.

" I swear the earth shall surely be complete to him or her who shall be complete!

" I swear the earth remains broken and jagged only to him or her who remains broken and jagged!"

So says the latest prophet of the years, and *truly* he says it. One doesn't realize it at first flush. It is so great, so mighty, that *you* and *I* can hardly understand that *we* are the ones, in particular, that the old man is talking about. And yet, so it is, and we *know* it, when we come to think about it. Surely, *so far as I am concerned*, the sun and moon hang in the sky for me especially. Drop *me* out of the account, and what odds is it to me whether there be any sun, moon, or whatsoever? And so on, to the end of all the old poet's words claim for us.

Now, it is this view of humanity that makes life worth living, for *me*. It is this infinite *individuality* and *personality* that is in *you* and in *me*, and in *everybody* (white, black, brown, or what you will), and which makes us all equals on the great plane of spiritual being — it is this thing that makes it seem worth while for me, or for you, or for anybody to live at all, and to labor and strive to move ourselves and the rest of the brethren on and up. It is this that makes *me* willing to sit down and write to *you*, and that will make it worth while for *you* to read what I write, if I say anything worth reading at all.

And, above all, it is this view of things that makes the public school worth while, and that puts the teacher's profession on the very topmost round of the ladder of human employments. And especially is this so in this great American democracy of ours, where we have undertaken to make the total average of humanity so high that to its hands can be safely entrusted the government of this mighty people, the settlement of such gigantic questions as time has never before produced, the development of a civilization that shall make all the former attainments of the nations of the earth sink into insignificance by way of contrast.

This is what we have undertaken to do, and if the attempt ever succeeds, it must be because the public schools make such success possible.

But if these schools ever perform the Herculean task that is demanded of them, it will be because they so adapt themselves to the million-and-one *personalities* of the children of this nation, that they enable them to grow and develop as God meant they should grow and develop, each and all, every one just as free to think and act as *you* are — not to think and act as *you* do, but as each one *personally* elects, after his own kind.

And, if this thing is ever done, it is *you* who have got to do it, so far as *you* are concerned ; it is *I*, it is *everybody*, but each one in particular.

And so the questions that force themselves upon *you*

and upon *me* are, what can *we* do ? How can *we* do it ? And, above all, *will we* do something, right now ?

Looking at the present status of the public schools, *you* know and *I* know that they are not now doing all that they should do, all that the requirements of the hour demand that they should do. We know that *we do not hold the great bulk of the children of the common people in these schools but a small percentage of the time that these same children ought to be under careful discipline and training.* How can we hold these pupils longer, and train them as they ought to be trained ? Long years of the most careful experiment have proved that we cannot do it as our schools are now fashioned, their curricula being what they now are. The question is, how can we do it ?

Or, what is far more to the point, how can *you* do it, beloved ? There's the rub. It is little or no odds to *you* and *yours* what the others do ; the item that should engage all *your* soul is, what can *I* do ? And what I beg for is, that *you* do *something* toward the solution of this momentous question in the special field in which *you* are working. I don't ask or urge you to do, or to try, anything radical. I beseech you not to try to solve the whole problem for the whole nation at one fell swoop. I beg of you not to seek for any wholesale or patent process that can be applied to all the schools in the country and instant relief be guaranteed to follow. From all these weaknesses of the flesh and wiles of the devil, good Lord deliver you — and us. But this I do suggest, that, things being as they are, *you* do what *you* can to better the situation in *your* immediate field of labor. Do that, *in your own way*, and great shall be your reward.

Anent which, a letter has just this minute reached me, just as I wrote the last sentence in the last paragraph. It comes from a teacher in Kansas, and a portion of it reads thus: "We teachers out here are struggling for more light on these great educational issues of the day. We are approaching these momentous problems cautiously, though fearlessly, and are bound to get at the true inwardness of them, so far as it is in our power to do so. We may get great knots of egotism and self-confidence and fossilized adherence to antiquated ideas knocked off from our hide-bound anatomies; but, if so, we will gather together what there is left of ourselves, and push forward to grander and better things."

There! That is the idea! It is just such a spirit as this that will break holes through all obscurities and let the light in, somehow. There will be mistakes made, of course there will; but such a steadfast purpose as the above words indicate cannot fail of yielding great results as time goes on. Don't *you* think so?

One more remark and I am done with this theme. Don't you see how all this means that *you* have got to be the final judge as to what it is best to do under the present circumstances? You may advise, and counsel, and read, and look up authorities, and watch what other people do, and all that; but if you ever do anything worth while for the cause, it will be in *your own way* — something that you have thought out yourself and are willing to try, because *you* believe there is something in it.

It will be in vain for you to imitate what others have done. Imitation is never of any account. As Mr. Emerson has it: "Imitation can never go above its level, and the imitator dooms himself to hopeless mediocrity from the very outset. The inventor did it because it was natural to him, but for any one else to do merely what he has done, this is the veriest of slavish servitude, out of which nothing good can come."

So don't imitate anything or anybody. It is written:

"Thou shalt not make unto thee a graven image. Thou shalt not bow down to them, nor serve them, for I, the Lord thy God, am a jealous God!" Yea, truly, it is so. So do not imitate.

But this you can do. You can get ideas from here, and there, wherever you get a chance to forage; and you can *adapt* these ideas, or ways and means, or what not, to *your* particular needs, and all this greatly to your advantage. It is Emerson who says again: "No genius is so great that it can afford to dispense with the experience of others." This is gospel truth, but see to it that you do not merely imitate under the guise of availing yourself of the experience of others. *Adapt everything; adopt nothing!* That is the rule to work by, and it will bring the best of results ever and always.

What I want to say is, that if you or I ever amount to anything on the tally-sheet of deeds in this world, it will be because we —

"Ordain ourselves, loosed of limits and imaginary lines.
"Going where we list — our own masters, total and absolute.
"Listening to others, and considering well what they say.
"Pausing, searching, receiving, contemplating —
"Nevertheless, gently, but with undeniable will divesting ourselves of the holds that would hold us, and doing our own work in our own way, as God meant we should do it even from the first."

Do this, my brother, my sister, *whoever you are*, and you shall be blessed of God. You may be cursed by men, but that will not count; for the benediction of heaven shall overwhelm all else, and bring you the perfect peace and joy which the whole world else can not bestow, and which, thank God, all the world can never take away from you. Do *you* believe this? And if you do, will you act in accordance with your belief? You need not answer me! *Will* you answer *yourself?*

This chapter is much more like a sermon than I intended it should be when I set out to put it in order. Nevertheless, the spirit said unto me, "Write!" and I have written.

AN OPEN BOOK.

Did *you* ever take a "Written Arithmetic" that has seen service, I don't care for how long, if only some one has "gone through" it one or more times, and, holding it up on its back between your two hands on the table before you, so that it stands perfectly perpendicular, suddenly release it, and notice where it will fall open? If you have never done this, suppose you try it, and perhaps it will put you on the track of something that you never thought of before.

Now I am neither a prophet nor the son of a prophet, but just so surely as you make this experiment I can foretell where the pages will part. The book will fall open, invariably, at the "Miscellaneous Problems" at the end of fractions.

I discovered this the other day while I was rumaging around in our attic, which is a sort of cemetery for dead books, whose graves it is a kind of melancholy pleasure to visit and linger over for a while, now and again, calling up old memories of this or that which these mummified pages once made a part of (what memories some of those yellow leaves do recall). I say, being thus engaged, I picked up a copy of Adams's old arithmetic (the first book of the kind that I ever sat up nights with), and as it accidentally slipped from my hand and fell upon the floor it opened as noted above. The pages that were exposed by this display were worn almost to shreds, and many of the problems were so begrimed with thumb-marks that they could scarcely be read, while the book, as a whole, was in a pretty fair state of preservation.

As I stood for an instant gazing at these as-it-were-footprints from my own paleozoic age, I fell to wondering why the book happened to open just there (I always was curious about things), and then it occurred to me that perhaps other arithmetics might duplicate the act, under similar circumstances.

So I turned to a row of arithmetical sarcophagi that stood on a shelf just before me (there was a long line of them, for some one has been going to school from our family most of the time for forty years, during a large share of which period those apostles of education, the school book agents, have been going about making changes and *change* wherever they went, and this row of mathematical coffins is the earnest of their faithful labors), and took down a copy of Greenleaf, which came next in order.

I set the book on its back on the floor, holding it straight up with my hand, and then suddenly "let loose," and — there it was, just the same as its predecessor! Then I tried Davies. There was neither variation nor shadow of turning in the result! Then came Colburn, and Ray, an 1 Robinson, and White, and a whole hecatomb of later fry, and in not a single instance did the sign fail. The demonstration was perfect, at least so far as our family was concerned.

But, like a true scientist that I am, I remembered that one swallow does n't make a summer, and it occurred to me that, perchance, this phenomenon might be a peculiar attachment of our family — so I set out to generalize from the individual concept, which had taken its initiative as above noted!

I went into the cellar of a down-town book store, about

a week after school began in the fall, and there I found a cord or more of "exchanged" arithmetics (books which, like Dead Sea fruit, had suddenly turned to ashes in the hands of the children, just as they were beginning to like them a little for old times' sake, if nothing else), and I took down a couple of dozen or so of these "back-numbers," and began to try experiments with them.

At first I picked up the books at random and tested them according to my theory, but presently it occurred to me that even *this* might not be a thoroughly infallible proof; for, without specially guarding the point, there was a *possibility* that all the books thus taken might belong to the children of some one nationality, and in these days of positive science, if a principle is worth its salt it must be established as world-wide in its application.

And so I got the idea of making a Pan-average-American-and-Foreign-born-school-child test of my hypothesis, and to this end I went through that pile of old paper and picked out books in which the following names were duly inscribed on the inside of the pasteboard covers (the "fly leaves" were missing in all the books I examined): Peter Brown, Solomon Isaacs, Patrick Murphy, Fritz Loutenheizer, Ignaccio Papionelli, Lars Larson, Ann Jones, Marie Chevalier, Jean McDonald, Topsy Johnson, Inez Dosamantes, and Catharine Trediakovitchiski, and with these I proceeded with my experimentation.

The result confirmed my most sanguine expectations; for, in every case, the openings were as before noted, and the pages exposed presented the same bedraggled and generally worn-out appearance that I had noticed in the first instance of the kind that came under my observation. *

* In behalf of scientific inquiry, it is due that I state that, in the experiments above mentioned, Solomon Isaacs' book seemed possessed of a secret longing to fall open at "Interest," while Topsy Johnson's evinced a disposition to open everywhere at once, but on a fair trial they both yielded to the greater pressure, and did really fall apart as I have reported.

And it is for these reasons that I feel justified in making the bold prophetic statement that occurs in the second paragraph of this chapter. I believe the fact to be verified, beyond question, that books such as I have described, treated as I have noted, will behave as I have herein said they would. And if this postulate is established, let us proceed to search for the cause of these remarkable phenomena - for such I certainly consider them to be.

Here, then, is the problem: Why is it that there is such singularity of eventuation, resultant from a uniformity of actuation exerted upon certain similar books which have previously been subjected to an apparently inconstant mode of manipulation? (As a scientist, I hold that, when dealing with scientific subjects, all the statements pertaining thereto should be couched in scientific terms).

Now, pursuing this investigation on the line of modern methods of research (I am myself a devout disciple of Bacon, and believe thoroughly in inductive ways of arriving at conclusions) the first thing to be done was to collect data from which, if possible, to establish a theory that should meet the requirements of the given proposition.

With this fundamental principle as the guiding star of my action, I set out for our garret again, there to resurvey the field of my primary observations.

On my way home I beguiled the weary horse-car half hour by reading an article on railroads in a current number of one of the great monthlies, and there I came across this sentence: "The rails on a heavy grade will last less than half as long as those on a level stretch of road, for it is a uniform principle, that, where the greatest amount of friction is, there will be found the greatest amount of wear and tear."

I am confident that it was the last three words in the sentence that threw my thought again into the channel of

my research; for it occurred to me, then and there, by that
natural sequence of ideas with which all psychological
students are so familiar, that all the pages which had been
disclosed in the books I had let fall open were literally
covered (what there was left of them) with undeniable
marks of both "wear and tear;" and from this point it was
but a step to the conclusion that such record must have
been produced by a "great amount of friction." Yea,
verily!

With this hint I got into the top room of our house
once more, and began to hunt for the friction-makers at
this particular place in all arithmetics that I know anything about. And I found them, galore! Hence this
chapter.

And, to make the case clear, I give herewith a few of
the retarding elements that I found, though some of them
were scarcely decipherable, owing to the great amount of
friction that had been exerted upon them. I have taken
them from the Miscellaneous-Problems-at-the-back-end of
fractions of several arithmetics, and have tried to select
them fairly, so as to truthfully represent the point I am
driving at. Thus, I read through the grime:

"In a certain orchard $\frac{1}{4}$ of the trees are peach, $\frac{1}{5}$ are
plum, $\frac{2}{7}$ are cherry, and the remaining III are apple; how
many trees in the orchard?"

"A can do a piece of work in 9 days, B and C can do
.t together in 5 days, and B can do $\frac{3}{4}$ as much as C. How
many days would it take them to do it, all working together?"

"The sum of two fractions is $\frac{7}{8}$, and their difference
is $\frac{2}{5}$; what are the fractions?"

"A fish's head is 10 inches long, its tail is as long as
its head and $\frac{1}{3}$ its body, and its body is as long as its head
and tail together; how long is the fish?"

But I need not extenuate, nor would I set down aught in malice. To be sure, the problems I have given above are the worst worn of any I found, and in some cases the "tear" in them was so great that I had to supply the figures, but neither of these things in any way affects the argument. *You* know that problems, of which the above are but accentuated specimens, abound at this point in all written arithmetics. *You* know what a time you had with them when you went over them; and still better do you know, as a teacher, what a time you have had with every class you have tried to put through them — or them •through your class!

If you grew up in a country school, you know that for winter after winter you sat in the back seat and scratched your head over these and similar problems; and if you were reared on the graded-school pian, you know that you labored on such examples night after night, and got all the folks in the house to help you solve them, and then did your best to remember *just how the figures looked on your slate,* so that you could reproduce them on examination, if you had to! In either case it took weeks to get over the two or three pages of these puzzlers, and hence the " wear and tear " that your old book doth show.

Now, the thing in all this that gives me pause is, how does it come about that arithmetic-makers put such problems as these in this part of the book? When you look these examples steadily in the face, and probe into their true inwardness, you cannot help asking what business have they here, anyhow? And the only answer I can possibly imagine as coming from anybody is this, that *they have fractions in them* and so belong in *that* department of arithmetic.

But what an answer is this! So does the calculation of any one of the occultations of Jupiter's moons have fractions in it, but that can hardly be urged as a good and sufficient reason why such a problem should have a place in Miscellaneous Problems in fractions in arithmetic! And yet such an argument would be but a few degrees more flinty than the one which would place such problems as I have quoted in this part of our school arithmetics.

The fact is that the fractional elements in these problems are mere trifling affairs as compared with the principles which the solution of these same problems involves. And as for these principles, when the pupil "tackles" these problems he has not been given one single word of instruction as to how to deal with them and their likes.

For instance, take the first problem I have quoted. It belongs to a *general class of problems* in which several parts of a quantity are noted, and a definite number is announced as being equal to the remainder that is left when all these several parts are put together and this sum is taken from the whole. But where, in his previous work, has the child come across anything even remotely resembling this? He has never been even so much as "exposed" to such a situation.

And all of the other problems I have quoted are open to the same criticism. Their solution demands a mastery of principles that belong to mathematics far in advance of the attainments of the pupils to whom such examples are given. And hence the friction. Talk about bricks without straw! An Israelite in Egypt with only a handful of Nile reeds out of which to make his daily tale of adobe, was plethoric in resources as compared with the destitute mathematical condition of the hordes of grammar school children who are driven, head on, to these problems, the country over, every day in the week!

But I would not care so much about that—I have no objection to having the children worked, and worked hard, in arithmetic; it is not about that, or anything like that, that I complain — but what I do rebel against is, the demoralizing outcome of such a method of procedure.

And that such is the result, you and I are living examples. These problems, and their likes, upset us, mathmetically, for many a day and year. They made guessers, and cut-and-try workers, and answer-hunters out of us. When they were put at us we didn't know whether to add, or subtract, or multiply, or divide; and so we tried first one of these processes and then the other or perhaps all four at once; and when we had it "figured through," we hastened to turn back to see if we had the answer!

Isn't that what these problems made *us* do, and do they not make your pupils do the same, even unto this day?

Now, if there is anything that mathematics ought to teach it is definiteness of design, clear perception of procedure, and certainty of results—in a word, *absolute accuracy* should be the purpose of all mathematical training. But the wrestling with problems like these, in the way we all have to—if they are given to us in our early teens and without a word of preparation for them—this tends to the very reverse of accuracy, and generates in us a looseness of thought and a dabbling with chances that drive us close into the realm of shams and pretense, not to say lying, before we are aware.

"What would I do about it?" I would cut every one of those problems out of the arithmetics, where they occur—that is so far as giving them to pupils is concerned. And then, when the boys and girls got so they could manipulate numbers well—could add, subtract, multiply, and divide whole numbers and fractions rapidly and accurately; when I was certain that they knew their multiplication table so well that they didn't have to keep the fore finger of their left hand in the book at that table whenever they were working problems, and could add without using their fingers for counters—when I was sure they had passed that period, then I would take up a STUDY OF PROBLEMS, *as such*, and pursue the subject with them intelligently, systematically, and definitely, till they mastered it.

For instance, the first problem I have quoted belongs to *a class of problems*, as I have already said. I would take up, say, that class, or kind of problems, beginning with very simple ones, and teach my pupils to see what was given, and how the same must be manipulated to find out what is required. *For all problems of this particular kind are worked in exactly the same way.*

And when my pupils had "caught the idea," I would improvise a hundred *similar* problems, all involving the same principle and worked in the same way, making the numbers larger, and the complications more and more intricate as we went along. And I would teach them to recognize problems of this class, no matter where they stand in the arithmetic.

Thus, there is no reason why this first problem should not have its fractional parts expressed as hundredths, and so find its place in decimal fractions, or percentage; but if a pupil had studied it *as a problem*, he would smile on it under any form, and solve it accurately, every time.

But without *a study of problems*, as such, when the like of this turns up in percentage it is a *new thing* to the average student, something to sweat over and guess at, even as when it first appeared in another guise.

But this chapter is already too long. I only add that everyone of these miscellaneous problems is capable of being relegated to its proper *class* and should be studied only in such company, and then by the batch. The-one-

of-a-kind-and-every-kind-different hodge-podge of examples that now makes up the part of arithmetic that always
shows its dirty face when an old book of this sort is permitted to parade itself, is a monstrosity that ought to be
banished from all healthy mathematical society.

Won't *you* help to shove it out into the rubbish pile,
where it ought to have gone long ago; or, better still,
won't *you* do what *you* can to land it in a perdition which it
amply deserves for having caused so much trouble in the
world — and for having led so many primarily honest
souls astray.

AMONG THE AZTECS.

Just as a preacher now-a-days, sometimes, after he
has read his text, begins forthwith to explain to his con-
gregation that the words he has read in their hearing do
not mean at all what they have commonly been supposed
to mean, but something entirely different ; that they
include more and exclude less, etc., etc., so I proceed to
remark to my " beloved readers" that the line-with-a-slot-
in-it, which has so kindly furnished me the theme for these
disjointed papers, should not be too literally construed
nor made too narrow in its application ; for it was my
original intention that it should be liberal enough in its
boundaries to permit my " Walks Abroad " to include
also my *rides*.

I make this remark for the sake of any literal critics
who may happen to read these lines, lest, in what follows,
they should insist that I could not have *walked* so far as I
presently shall speak of going; and that, having misrepre-
sented in one case, I am not to be believed in any.   For

does **not the** law clearly say, *falsus in uno falsus in omne ;* and does not the challenging of the authority of law lead directly to anarchy, as the questioning of doctrine and dogma leads, head on, to infidelity ? These things must be looked after, or, as Mr. Dickens says, " the country is done for."

How could we live without literal critics ?

And so I state again, to make sure that there may be no danger of misunderstanding, that, true to the Hibernian instinct which has always been strong within me, when I say "walks" I mean "rides"; that these terms are synonymous in my thought and mutually controvertible in my expression, and I shall do my very best to keep them equal in power and glory.

And now, if we understand each other, we will go on.

In one of my "walks abroad," the other day, I got as far away from home as the City of Mexico, and the things I saw while there are enough to fill the blank place in my line-of-the-missing-link for many and many a day.

I think the thing that impressed me most during my stay in the old city was the fact that I found I knew so little about it before I got into it. And yet I studied my geography, all right and regular, and I find, on referring to my diploma (which I have looked up for this very purpose, it being the first time I have had occasion to use it since it was granted, twenty-five years ago). that my mark in this branch of learning for the term which included the study of Mexico was 96 !

Surely I must have known something about this region once, or, in any event, I must have succeeded in making my teacher think that I knew something of it, or, at least, in making her think that it would be a good thing

4

to make other people think that I knew — for the records were open to inspection, and my diploma is addressed, " To all the World, Greeting ! "

But the truth is, I knew very little of Mexico as it is when first I set foot on her soil.

As near as I can make out, what ideas I had of this country were gathered from the geography study which my diploma kindly preserves the memory and record of. As far as my own recollection of that epoch in my school life is concerned, I find a sort of a shadowy remembrance of some pretty tough lessons, near the back part of the book, where there were pictures of savages and heathen sparsely clad in hot weather clothes, and living in bamboo huts ; and, arranged around which pictures aforesaid, were certain strings of letters which were alleged to be the names of something, but which seemed to my boyish vision like a transcript of zig-zag lightning with the kinks all left in.   Witness Iztaccihuatl, Huitzilopochtli, Acama-pitzin, Itztli, etc., etc.

A page or two of that sort of thing must have been a most delectable diet of mental pabulum to set a " maw-crammed and crop-full" boy down to, as, sleepily, he began to turn the pages before him about half an hour after school "took up " after dinner !

The geography class always recited after dinner. I don't know why it was, but somehow geography always was an afternoon study.   We read and did arithmetic in the morning, when we were fresh, but grammar and geography always came in the afternoon.   Perhaps that is the reason I remember so little about these two studies, though my marks in both of them are very high.   I was always a pretty good guesser, and I early learned that if a noun came *after* the word " is " it was in the " nominative case after " and not " objective after," and so my grammar marks were as good as those in geography.

I have forgotten, though, how it happened that my geography marks were so good. But I know that they were good, for my diploma says so, and the figures on it are all made by a man who wrote a most beautiful hand. You ought to see those figures ! I hadn't seen them for twenty-five years till to-day, but truly they are beautiful !

"But, to return to our subject," as our dear pastor says.

My friend, Prof. —— (fill it in to suit yourself, you all know him), who sits in his library reading this article, and who tells his children to "go and find mother and talk to her" if they happen to come into the room where he sits by himself, surrounded by his books, and reads, and reads, and reads,— remarks just here :

" But why did he have to rely on the memory of the geography he learned at school for his knowledge of Mexico before he visited that country ? Has he, then, never read Prescott's 'Conquest of Mexico,' nor Brantz Mayer's 'History of the Mexican War,' nor Kingsborough's 'Mexican Antiquities,' nor any of the classic authorities on this most interesting people and their *habitat* ? "

To whom I reply .

My dear sir, I have not read these books, not one of them. I wish I had, but, to be honest with you, I haven't. And if you want to know why I haven't, I beg to explain that, up to the time I was of age I lived on a farm, mostly, where we got up before day-light the year round, and "hustled" from the hour when the "rosy-fingered Aurora appeared bringing back the dawn" till after supper, when we were too tired to do anything but go to bed.

That is one reason why I didn't read these interesting books in the days of my youth, and another reason is, that our folks didn't have these books, nor many others, even if I had had time to read them. And I further respectfully submit that, in this respect, I much resemble about 95 per cent. of the boys (and girls, too, for that matter) who attend our public schools!

To be sure, these do not all grow up on farms; but they do live in homes where there is no plenitude of wealth; where all the household has to work hard at manual labor for a living, and where there are few books on Mexico or any other country. That is how it happens that I was forced " to rely on the memory of the geography I learned at school for my knowledge of Mexico before I went there," and why there are several millions of people in this dear land of ours who would be obliged to do the same thing, should they take the " walk abroad " which I have recently taken.

This shows why we ought to have pretty good geographies in our schools.

But to return once more to our subject.

I was surprised to find that one of the things I did not know about the City of Mexico was what a perfectly delightful climate it has. I don't remember one word about "climate" in the geography, unless it might have been " mild and salubrious." But those words are of no manner of account in giving one an idea of the climate of Mexico City. They can't begin to do the subject justice. Let me tell you a thing or two, and then see if you think they are equal to the emergency.

We got into the City of Mexico about the middle of January, and we left it the first of March, and if we saw a cloud in the sky bigger than Barnum's circus tent during all that time, I have forgotten it. Six weeks of sunshine without a break! And I was told by perfectly reliable parties that it had been just that way ever since the first of October, and that that was the regular thing, every year, infallibly.

That is to say, from October to March it never rains in Mexico City. The sun shines continually (I mean by *day*, dear literal critic) for more than five months in the year, and umbrellas can go to the pawnshop all that time, so far as rainy weather is concerned.

In early April the rains begin, and they come decently and in order. In the first place, they always come in the afternoon. It never rains in the morning in Mexico City. The showers come at about five o'clock in the afternoon, and they are generally over by seven. Sometimes they last till into the night, but not often. The mornings are always bright, and a fellow always has a fair chance to get his work done, every day, before the rain begins.

During June, July and August, it rains every day, from five to seven p. m., and no postponements on account of the weather. By October 1st the rains are over, and they can be absolutely relied upon not to show up again till the following April.

Now, that is what I call a good weather programme, so far as the hydraulic part of it is concerned. As to the heat, that is equally satisfactory. The mean temperature for the year is 65 degrees Fahrenheit. The hottest month is May, when the thermometer sometimes reaches 85 degrees. The coldest month is August, when the mercury gets as low as 50 degrees. During our stay, from January to March, the hottest weather we saw was 75 degrees, and the coldest 55 degrees.

Can "mild and salubrious" do justice to such a climate as that? I wonder, too, if these facts had been noted in my geography if I should not have remembered them, whether I got 96 or not.

But I must draw rein, for, once on this subject of the climate of Mexico City, I shall write on to the end of the book if I don't put a limit on myself.

And even then I could not tell of *all* its charms. How the farmers have six rainless months in which to gather their crops, and no harm to fear for their grain. How they have more than four months to plant in, and yet their crops all come up together and get ripe together; because, you see, about the first of December the ground gets so dry that grain will not sprout in it, even though it is planted, but will lie there, safe and sound, till the rains come, and then all come up at once, and grow evenly, and get ripe evenly. Oh, there are a thousand things to tell, just about *this*, but "time and space forbid."

That is not the way my geography lesson about Mexico ended. I wish it had been. Because, then, I might have been so much interested in what I learned about that country in school that I should have read about it in "Classic Authorities" when I got where I could.

THE SCHOOLS OF MEXICO.

I came across a good many other things not set down in geography, during my "walks abroad" in that so-near-and-yet-so-far sister Republic, and there are not a few of them, of an educational nature, which seems to me worthy of mention in this record.

In the first place, as we were on our way down to Vera Cruz, I happened, by one of those fortunate accidents which every now and then will come to even the most unlucky of mortals, to make the acquaintance of a gentleman who, above all others, could give me the "inside track," so to speak, that led to the very "upper walks" in Mexican education circles. This was none other than Señor Sandoval, of the state of Zacatecas, the man who was chairman of the committee appointed by President Diaz to determine the nature and extent of the educational exhibit which the Republic of Mexico made at the World's Fair, in Chicago.

It was a little curious, too, how I happened to "locate" this most excellent and worthy Mexican scholar, teacher, and above all, gentleman.

Our train had stopped in the "bush" (for we were down in the low country) for some unexplained reason, and everybody was curious to know the "why" of this unexpected phenomenon. Windows went up all along the cars, on both sides of the train, and as many heads were thrust out through them as though the geography of the event were Massachusetts instead of the "*terra caliente*" of old, and reputedly incurious Mexico.

Strange, isn't it, how, the world over, we all flatter

ourselves that we are the only ones who do this or that; till presently, walking abroad, we find everybody doing the very thing we thought we had a corner on? The Mexicans on that train were as curious a lot of men and women as though they had been born under the shadow of Bunker Hill Monument.

But, as I was saying, when the train stopped, a very urbane Mexican gentleman got up from his seat behind me, and stood in the aisle, just beside me, looking out to see what he could see. In his hand he held a book; and, as he leaned over, I trained enough of my newly acquired Spanish into line to make out that the volume was none other than Mr. Herbert Spencer's Essay on "Education," translated into Spanish, and published by those worthy bookmakers, D. Appleton & Co. of New York.

Now, experience has taught me that the books a man reads are a far better index to his character than a whole carload of certificates, recommendations and diplomas on the same point; and as soon as I saw this book in the hands of this gentleman, I felt, instinctively, that I had found a friend, if only I knew enough to speak with him in his native tongue.

Great was my delight, therefore, when, a moment later, I discovered that, although I was unable to speak Spanish with this gentleman he was thoroughly prepared to speak English with me; for, turning to me, he asked a question in words and tone that even "Fair Harvard" might not have been ashamed of. To this I made reply to the best of my ability, and a few minutes later we were chatting together just as easily as if we had grown up in the same door yard, instead of having been born several thousand miles apart, one a native Mexican, and the other just as native a Yankee. It was the books we had read that thus brought us together. It is always so.

As our conversation progressed, I soon found that my newly acquired acquaintance was exceedingly well posted on educational topics, both ancient and modern, foreign and domestic; and I judged him to have been the very man for the place, in mapping out the matter and manner of the Mexican educational exhibit, in Chicago.

He gave a brief outline of what he had done, but I was specially anxious to hear from him, direct, as to the present status of education in the Republic. On this subject he was, of course, well prepared to speak, and he gave me much interesting and valuable information regarding the same; but, what was infinitely better, he gave me a chance to see for myself, by telling me where I could find the best schools in Mexico, and by giving me letters of introduction which I found to be limitless passports into the very heart of Mexico's educational 400.

For the very acme of courtesy and genuine good fellowship, commend me to a Mexican gentleman and scholar of the type of Señor Sandoval. What a pleasure it is to know that there are the best of good men, all over the earth.

Being thus introduced, the school I saw the most of was the National Normal School, located in the City of Mexico, of which Señor Serrano is Director General.

Regarding this school, let me say, first, that it is the special pet of President Diaz, who has done everything for it that money and an enthusiastic friend could do. This peer among the greatest of modern statesmen is thoroughly a nineteenth century man, and he believes that the thing above all others that Mexico needs, just now, is a public school system that shall educate *all her people;* and, as a first step in that direction, he has built up this National Normal School which is intended to prepare teachers for their work in the schools of the Republic.

How well he has succeeded in making the materialization of his plan tally with his ideal may be gathered, in part, from what follows.

The school is compose of two divisions, one for young men and the other for young women, the practice of co-education of the sexes not having reached Mexico. These different divisions occupy separate buildings, which are several blocks apart; and, as a matter of fact, are as independent of each other as though they had not a common aim. I visited only the school for young men, and all I have to say is about that branch of the institution.

I found, upon inquiry, that, while President Diaz fully believes in the co-education of the sexes, yet he does not deem it wise to attempt such a measure in a country where prejudice is so deeply rooted and so strongly set against it.

Indeed, the prudent policy of this man, not only in this, but in a hundred other matters, commanded my profoundest respect, the more I learned of him and his doings in the last twenty years. He is a man among men who really believes that Rome was not made in a day, and who has the patience and good sense to regulate his actions accordingly. If he lives twenty years longer, and remains at the head of affairs in Mexico during that period, he will have Mexican boys and girls learning their lessons seated in the same school-room; but if he ever does bring about such a state of things, it will be because he has head enough not to be in too big a hurry about it!

I wonder if it would be possible for some of *our* "get-there" Americans to learn anything from this patient and business-like head of the Mexican Republic.

The building occupied by the young men's department of this school is located near the Palace buildings, just a little off from the Zocalo, or chief square of the city.

It is a two story structure, and built around the four sides of a central square, or *patio*, after the manner of all Mexican buildings. When Diaz came into power this building was an old monastery; but, in common with hundreds of similar structures, it was confiscated by the republic, and is now state, rather than church property.

And may I stop, just here, to say that the church and the state are most thoroughly divorced from each other in modern Mexico, under the rule of Diaz. This separation is carried to such an extent that no religious exercises whatever are permitted in connection with any state affairs; nor is a priest, or a nun or a protestant minister, or even a "Y. M. C. A. young man" allowed to go upon the street clad in garments that in any way indicate his or her relations to religion or the church—any church.

On the street, all men are alike, in that they are then simply citizens of the Republic. In their homes, or in their churches, they may dress as they please and do as they will, provided they keep within bounds; but in public, their peculiar creeds or whatnot peccadillos must not be flaunted in the faces of their neighbors.

Any church—all churches, *per se*, receive the fullest protection from the Mexican government. A Mormon or a Hotentot can go there and worship according to the dictates of his own conscience, and the whole power of the Mexican government is behind him as a guarantee that he shall in no way be molested or made afraid, so long as he "keeps out of politics;" but let any church or religious organization, as such, begin to meddle with state affairs, and somebody is exceedingly liable to be in states'-prison, forthwith.

Curious, some of the ways they have in Mexico!

The building fronts on a well kept street, and is built flush to the side walk. Its only entrance or exit is a wide door which is in the middle of the building, on the street side, and there is always a *portero*, or guard, on duty there. Every pupil and teacher has to pass this guard in going in or out; and an accurate record is kept of the presence or absence of everybody connected with the school, during school hours. This record is preserved, and is open to inspection, to all parties concerned, at any and all times. In this and some other respects there is a rigorous military discipline in the management of this school.

I found Señor Serrano, the president of the institution, to whom I presented my letter of introduction, a most gracious and affable gentleman. He is about sixty-five years old, and has "seen service," as nearly every prominent Mexican has who has reached that age and has had anything to do with public affairs. He was for many years a successful lawyer, and was called to his present position on account of his rare executive ability. He was director in chief of the Mexican exhibit in Chicago and spent most of his time in that city during the progress of the Fair. I found him dictating a letter to Mrs. Potter Palmer on some point connected with the exhibit he had charge of, and in which she was also interested, and if that lady ever receives a more dignified, gracious and diplomatic epistle than that same letter, like the author of John Gilpin, "may I be there to see."

My letter of introduction was a "sesame open" to the school and all that pertained thereto, and I spent some two days in going about the institution, which is, in many respects, much like a normal school in "the states;" but which has a number of things, that, like somebody's sarsaparilla, are "peculiar to itself."

There are about two hundred young men in the school preparing to teach. The course covers four years, and is considerably more extended than that of any other normal school with which I am acquainted. It differs from our normal school course in that it has more language study than our schools insist on. Of these languages, Latin, French, German and English (and of course Spanish), all have prominent places; but it struck me as a significant fact that English is the *one* language, besides Spanish, the study of which is made compulsory.

Most of the teachers in the school speak English, and all of them are busy studying that language. Señor Serrano himself had never learned the English language though he speaks Spanish, French, and German; but the fact that he was to go to Chicago made him, as he said to me, "ashamed to go to a country the language of which he should be unable to speak," and so at sixty-five, he was learning English!

And admirably he was progressing, too, as his conversation showed, though he had been at work on it less than two months when I met him. As I compared my six weeks old Spanish with his English, which was but two weeks its senior, I was fain to hide my head and exclaim, "O, wretched man that I am, how can I catch the trick of learning a foreign language to equal this charming old gentleman!"

But from what I saw of Mexican students they are much quicker in learning a foreign language than our American students are. Indeed, the "cultured classes" in Mexico are much more proficient in speaking languages other than their mother tongue than are a corresponding set of people in the states. It is a rare thing to meet a scholarly person in the City of Mexico who does not speak more than one language, while it is not uncommon to meet men and women who will converse fluently in either Spanish, French, English, or German.

From what I observed, I think this is due partly to a natural bent of mind, suited to language study, which the Mexicans possess; but, perhaps more than this it comes from the *natural methods* of teaching a foreign language which are used in the Mexican schools. These are largely inductive, and consist in making pupils actually *talk* the language they are studying, rather than merely teaching them rules about how to talk if they ever get so they can! The signs of the times begin to indicate that similar methods will, before long, be largely used in the study of foreign languages in our own schools; and when they are, perhaps our children will show up as well in this branch of learning as the Mexican children do now.

MEXICAN CLASS-ROOM WORK.

As a workman is known by his chips, so is a school known by the pupils it turns out. This is universally true, but I make a special application of the principle in the case of the National Normal School, of the City of Mexico.

And, so far as Normal Schools are concerned, experience leads me to believe that the place to look for its "chips" is in the "model school," or "training department" of these institutions. The students of the normal schools proper become mere repositories, or storage batteries, as it were, of the theories and arts of the professors under whom they learn their trade. But in the training department one gets a view of ultimates — of the way in which these theories and arts "pan out," as a cold and heartless money-making man-o'-the-world would say.

Being aware of this fact, I spent small time in viewing the elegant laboratories and other mechanical appliances for making teachers with which this institution is so thoroughly equipped. All these are worth while, doubtless; but I felt as though I would be willing to "infer" considerable along these lines, if only I could get my eye on the "finished product" of the concern. And so I made straight for the model school, being once fairly in possession of *carte blanche* to the institution.

I found a school of nearly three hundred pupils, of all grades, from the primary up to the "higher branches," as in such cases made and provided. The school was well organized, and the greatest of care was exercised not to permit the crude efforts of "pupil teachers" to result harmfully upon the innocents on whom they "practiced."

This was a thing that pleased me greatly, because I have known instances where it was not done, and where the children who were worked upon by these "'prentice hands"—the chips—were terribly chopped up by the performance.

I know a young man to-day who cannot read a page in a magazine aloud, decently, but who can "elocute" anything he has learned by heart in a most charming manner; and all because, when he learned to read, in the training department of a normal school, under a pupil teacher who was let loose upon him without a chaperone, he was made to rehearse the same reading lessons over, and over, and over again, so that he could "*read them elegantly without looking at his book*," as his teacher used artlessly to say, when his class came up for examination before the whole school.

You see, this pupil teacher was marked on the work she did with this class, and the proof of her work was a show performance of her reading class before the whole school. And what so good a *show* as a nice, clean class of little folks, all dressed in their best clothes, standing in a row, reading, oh so charmingly, from books held in the left hand, and which they *didn't have to look at at all?*

And this was called teaching reading.

The woman who did this thing told me, recently, that, now she has come to realize the enormity of her work with that class, she has never dared even to pray for forgiveness; and whenever she meets one of the pupils whom she so ignorantly abused, she is fain to call on the rocks and mountains to fall upon her!

Perhaps her "punishment to fit her crime" may some time be to sit for ages and ages, and be compelled to listen to the stumblings and haltings of persons whose instruction in this branch of learning has been elocutionary drill to the neglect of sight reading!

But then, in all professions it is apt to be pretty hard on the patients of the ones who are learning the trade. Who was that celebrated surgeon that performed a very delicate and critical operation upon a lady's eye, and who, being complimented on his marvelous skill, replied: "Oh, but you should see the bushels of eyes I ruined while learning to be so skillful!"

And so I was glad to find the greatest of care in the supervision of the pupil teachers in this school.

As I have already said, the course is four years, and the normal students are not permitted to teach at all in the training department until the last half of the second year; and it is not until the fourth year that they are permitted to have entire charge of a class, and hear recitations unattended by some professor of the school. This guards the danger very well; and, judging from what I saw, reduces the evil well toward the vanishing point.

But some of the ways of this school are things to smile at, from our point of vision. For instance, in most of the rooms I visited in the training department, where recitations were going on, the teacher was smoking his cigarette as he heard the boys recite; and, not to distract his attention too much from his work, he had one of the boys of the school standing near at hand, whose business it was to "scratch a match" for him whenever his cigarette went out, or he wished to light a fresh one.

To perform this service for the teacher was a great honor rather than a disgrace, and in some of the rooms, at least, I learned that it was the special prerogative of the best boy in the school to thus be a torch bearer for his chief.

It was also interesting to me how this position of best-boyship was determined in some of the rooms. I do not know how general the method is, but this was the *modus operandi* in at least one room I visited:

The teacher gives the pupils, from time to time, and for various credits, bits of paper called *vales*, much like "rewards of merits" that we used to get "in the old days when I was young." Now when a boy becomes the lawful possessor of a number of these *vales*, they are his, to do with as he pleases; and here is what he pleases to do with them:

Everybody gambles in Mexico, and the boy who aspires to become the best boy in school resorts to this practice to gain the coveted position. And this is the way of it: If he happens to be a clever reader, for instance, he will challenge some member of his class to a reading match, each party to the contest to "put up" an agreed number of *vales* to "come into the game," as it were, and then they "read for the pile!"

The teacher is also made *particeps criminis*, and to him is given the position of umpire, or referee; though upon this condition, that, if *both* boys succeed in reading the

5

lesson perfectly, then the teacher must give to each of them a number of *vales* equal to the total number they have both together risked. If one boy trips, and the other does not, then the successful one "wins the pile;" while if both fail, the teacher "rakes in the stakes."

In this way the position of best-boy-in-the-school is striven for, and in this way only can it be won, for the boy who has the greatest number of *vales* at the end of each month is the best boy in school!

But, once won, like other high positions which are gained by equally creditable means in more countries than Mexico, great is the power and glory thereof. For, not only can the best boy in school light cigarettes for his teacher, but he becomes the monitor of the school room when the teacher is hearing recitations.

And so, between match scratchings the best boy patrols the aisles of the school room, calling the other boys to order, here and there as occasion requires, and recording in the note book, which the teacher furnishes him for such purpose, the delinquencies and shortcomings of any who fail to heed his warnings and exhortations to correct behavior. And from the record he makes there is no appeal. The teacher will sustain it, every time, as why should he not, for is it not the handiwork of the best boy in school!

Another perquisite of this high office of best boy is, that at the end of every month he is given all the tops, marbles, balls, knives, kite-strings, and whatsoever the the teacher or monitor has taken away from bad boys during the four weeks previous.

How different all this is from what we are used to here in the states. In this civilized land our teachers talk to the children about virtue being its own reward, and other unattractive maxims of similar import. But what inducements are these to make one strive for the position of best boy in school; and who can tell what might be, even here, if a conglomorate pile of tops, and balls, and marbles, and kite-strings, and whatsoever were held before the eager eyes of our children as the prize to be awarded at the end of every month to the fellow who could win the most *vales* from his schoolmates and teacher?

And then think of the emoluments of office that would rise to one's vision under such circumstances. Once installed as monitor, with autocratic power, what job lots of tops and balls, etc., one might confiscate from the bad boys, in the full assurance that they would be placed where they would do the most good at the end of the month! If that school does not turn out a full quota of Quays, or Wanamakers, or Brices, or Jay Goulds, one of these days, then shall I loose my faith in the power of educational training to mould character!

But, for all this — which seems to us so strange — I never saw better class-work, anywhere, than I saw in the training department of this normal school in Mexico. The pupils were alert, prompt, obedient, and interested.

I heard one recitation in mental arithmetic which was specially pleasing to me. It was a class of boys about twelve years old. The teacher stood before them and extemporized problem after problem, which involved the special principle upon which they were then working, which happened to be finding the area of rectangles, of varied dimensions, with such complications as this: "How many stone slabs, three feet long and two feet wide, would it take to pave a court thirty feet long by eighteen feet wide?"

As soon as the problem was announced the little fellows, every one of them, went at it with knitted brows, all the work being done mentally.

And it was wonderful how rapidly they found correct results. When a number had "raised hands" the teacher called on some one to solve the problem orally. The pupil would rise in his place and first salute the teacher by bringing his left hand to his forehead, and then waving it forward, at the same time making a slight bow; and then he would say, "Señor, what are your commands?" and then go on and solve the problem. There were some mistakes, but the work as a whole was most excellent.

To make sure that the work was not altogether a "put up job" for the entertainment and delectation of visitors, I asked the privilege of myself dictating a problem. This was most courteously granted, and the result showed that the instruction reached to principles, and was something more than mere parrot-like surface work.

In a word, the *teaching* done in this school struck me as being as excellent in its results as any I have ever seen, anywhere.

The school is semi-military, also, and all the pupils have uniforms which they wear on special occasions. Such occasions are frequent, as holidays, fete days, and the like, are "as thick as blackberries" in Mexico.

But even this is made of much service to the boys who attend this school; for, in order that they may be neat and trim looking in their uniform, and when on parade, they are held to the most rigid training regarding their personal apparel and appearance every day at school. Their faces and hands must be clean, their hair well kempt, their clothes brushed, and their shoes blacked *every day.* They are also held rigidly accountable for all the belongings assigned to their care in connection with their school work — their books, gymnasium outfit, gun, etc., all of which tends to most excellent training, according to my way of thinking.

It was a fine sight to see these three hundred or more boys, from six to fifteen years of age, pay a visit to Diaz, as they did on one of the days of late February or early March. They came to school at the usual hour, eight in the morning, all in uniforms, and as trim and neat looking as proud and ambitious mothers could make them.

At the armory they received their guns, and what can make a boy every inch a king equal to giving him a gun to carry?

And every one, even the smallest, had his gun.

Then they formed into line, about half-past eight, when, for some reason that I did not learn (perhaps it was part of the plan, just to try the boys), there was a halt in the proceedings; and for three mortal hours those boys stood in line, though the sun was hot and beat directly down upon them. It was a trying ordeal, surely. But the boys stood it bravely, and for the most part held their places in good form during all the slow passing hours.

Finally, a little before twelve they got the word to move, and away they went, a regimental band from Chatultepec leading them, marching to the president's home, which is about a mile from the school. Arrived there, they were admitted to the residence, and the whole line passed in review before the president, who shook hands with every boy of them as they went by. Then they marched back to school, where they broke ranks and went home for the day, having been steadily in service for between five and six hours.

Somehow I could not rid myself of the impression that this experience was one that would be of lasting value to the boys, in more ways than I can stop here to tell.

This association of President Diaz with the children of Mexico is a favorite act of his, and one of the means he uses to keep himself in touch with the common people. Thus, when the schools of the city closed the fall term, a little before Christmas, a grand assemblage of all the pupils of all the schools was held in the Alemeda for the awarding of prizes, some 60,000 children being present. The park was elaborately decorated with flowers, and there were speeches and singing, etc., etc. Diaz presided, and with his own hand delivered the prizes to the proud and happy victors.

The president has succeeded in securing the passage of a " compulsory attendance " law for the City of Mexico, and it is rigidly enforced, the police of the city being the truant officers thereof. This calls for large additions to the school accommodations, but these are rapidly being met under the skillful management of this marvelous head of the Mexican government.

In a word, Mexico is rapidly coming to the front educationally, as she is in other lines, and the magic name that has conjured all these changes among what was supposed to be a changeless people is Porfirio Diaz. Long life to him !

" THE ONLY.'

Leaving Mexico to the tender mercies of her present president, I turn my "walks abroad" once more into a territory nearer home, where there are still multitudes of men and things to "see" and talk about. In passing, however, there is one reflection that comes to me from a remark that I frequently heard while on Mexican soil: "What would become of Mexico if Diaz should die, and who would take his place?"

This is a question worth asking, surely, and one that the citizens of that republic need to keep well in mind; but the thought occurs to me that, should Diaz suddenly be taken away, some one would be found who both could and would take his place, with many chances to one in favor of doing so successfully, great and able man though the present president surely is.

Because, the fact is, that duplicates in any line of manhood are not nearly so hard to find in these days as they used to be in the times when kings and other dignitaries were supposed to be "the only" and truly great. Democracy has given many a heretofore hidden human light a chance to shine in the world, and it is amazing how brilliant some of these latent luminaries have become.

Indeed, it is no longer safe for anybody to declare himself as "the only," for, as soon as he does so, some one not only steps up and contests the validity of his claim, but plucks his blushing honors from him before he has time to say "who are you?"

Why, I can remember, a couple of years or so ago, when Zimmerman made a "world's record" on his wheel,

which record was somewhere about 2:40, and we all envied
him his marvelous feat, and wondered if there could ever
be another like him! But he had hardly got his wind
after this greatest effort of his life, before along came
Windle and lowered the record, a half-dozen seconds or
so, at one fell stroke; and then some one else put *him* into
the background in the course of a week or ten days — some
heretofore unheard of fellow from Omaha, or Minneapolis,
or some other backwoods town in the wild and wooly
west; a Swede, I think he was; anyhow, one out of the
great unknown — making a score clear and clean inside
the two-minute notch, and no one dares now to predict
how long even this limit will remain an ultimatum.

And so far as that first "world's record" is concerned,
the one we all once gaped at, I saw a "scrub race" of
boys, the other day, in which there were lads scarcely yet
in their teens who eclipsed it by some seconds.

Great is the stimulating power of a brilliant example
in the presence of uncurbed human ambition, and a fair
show and a free fight for everybody.

Nay, more than this, the infection seems to have
spread even to the brute creation, for Maude S. is no
longer Queen of the Turf, and John L. has forfeited his
right and title to the Championship of the World!

And so, I say, I suppose that, if Mr. Diaz should suddenly die, some one would be found who would take his
place, and perhaps eclipse even his brilliant and able
record. "The Lord advances and ever advances; always
the shadow in front, but always the reached hand of the
Almighty moving up the standard."

My reason for saying all this is the fact that, in my
walks abroad, now and again, I have observed divers and
sundry people (and among them not a few school teachers,
hence this record in this particular place) who seem

possessed with the idea that, in their several places and positions, they are "the only," and that everything with which they are now connected would at once go to the " demnition bow-wows " if, for any reason, they should be called upon, or compelled, to step down and out, so that the places which now know them should know them no more forever.   But let these, *et id omne genus*, grow modest in the presence of the facts which I have just noted.

The truth is that there is no one man, or any set of men, who carry this world either on their shoulders or in their pockets ; and, in the main, the wheels will keep on turning, right along, just as God has set them to turn, and neither you, nor I, nor any of the rest of the neighbors, are such important parts of the plan that, if we should drop out, the whole concern would go to smash.

I take it that the philosophy of all this lies in the fact that, in the eternal order of things, continual progress is the everlasting law of existence ; and, since this is so, whenever one becomes "the only," he has reached a finality beyond which he will not go, because he does not care to do so – does not have to do so.   And what one does not have to do in this world he is apt to leave pretty thoroughly alone.

And so this, "the only," state of mind leads any soul that it possesses into the ways of death.   It makes one arrogant, domineering, bull-dozing.   It is an attempt to nullify the second commandment, which says to mankind, " Thou shalt not make unto thee a graven image," that is, something that never changes.   And when one becomes " the only," in his own estimation or anybody's else, the graven image epoch has arrived ; and when that comes the sooner the turn is called the better.

And it will be called, so let us be modest.

Nearly every strike that has ever been inaugurated

has had, as a main factor in its theory of its ability to succeed, the idea that the strikers were "the only," and that no one could be found in all the world who could do the work that they were doing. The failure of the great bulk of these new phases of modern warfare shows how greatly mistaken the people are who are possessed of this fatuitous notion.

Doubtless we are great, but we are not "the only" great.

———

"SPECIALTY BUSINESS."

I went to a play with a friend, a few evenings ago, and we saw a lot of "Specialty Business," as it was put down on the bill. I had never seen it before, and for the most part I enjoyed it very much.

After the performance was over, my companion and myself went to his room, and there we fell to talking about what we had just seen. It transpired that he had seen the company a great many times and was well posted on their "business," and I very soon found that we had sat the evening through with entirely different degrees of pleasure. My friend remarked upon this, and finally went on to say:

"That's one trouble with this 'specialty' work and why it so soon grows stale; you see it a few times, and you see all there is in it, and after that it loses its charm for you. There wasn't a single new thing to me in that whole bill to-night, and I should have come out at the end of the first act if I hadn't seen that it was all new to you, and you were enjoying it so much."

I thanked him for his kindness, and then he went on:

"But, the fact is, this same sort of thing afflicts all

actors, more or less. There was Barrett, who had his specialty of skipping up the incline of a rising inflection to the very top round of the ladder of tone, when he wished to produce a startling stage effect ; and he had a trick of perching on the very pinnacle of a climax till the audience had to ' shoo ' him off with applause, as it were. And there was McCullough who, on the other hand, would go down, like McGinty, to the bottom of the vocal sea, whenever he was fathoming a strong dramatic situation. But these were tricks, both of them. And they all have them."

And then he cited Clara Morris, who always threatens to " skewer her brains " with a hair pin, no matter what the play may be ; and Maggie Mitchell, who never fails to put the end of her bonnet string in her mouth ; and Pat Rooney, who would always preface an encore with an address to the orchestra : " Put me up a few bars while I catch my breath," — and so on, till our cigars were out, and we went to bed.

After I got to bed, I fell to thinking of what my friend had said, and I very soon discovered that actors are not alone in this offending ; for I remembered that I had heard preachers who must needs plead guilty to the same charge, and some teachers, even, who would have trouble in proving an *alibi* if brought to trial on this count.

I remembered, too, that I had heard Mr. Beecher use the same illustration four several times, on four different occasions, and each time when speaking on a theme entirely different from that which formed the subject of his discourse when I heard him use the figure before.

And then I became dimly conscious of certain sins of my own, of a similar nature ; but the subject was not pleasant ; and as I always like to go to sleep happy, I did my best to think of something else, and succeeded so well that I was shortly dreaming as an honest man should.

The next day I went to a teachers' institute in a little, common-size country town, and, strange to say, I came across the same thing there again.

The institute was made up of a wholesome and healthy lot of country school teachers, marms and masters, and was much of the same sort as you can hit upon almost any Saturday, between September and June, in any one of the forty-four states of this glorious Union of ours.

The county superintendent was in charge, and he was ably flanked by a professor who has done institute work for several years. The latter was, of course, in the very nature of things, "cocked and primed" for the occasion, which was all very well and good ; but before I had sat in his presence five minutes I found he was working his "specialty business" for all that it was worth, and more, too. But I didn't object to this so much, remembering how, the night before, I had come to the conclusion that the disease was wide-spread.

Before long, however, I found myself rebelling against what was going on, and I herew.th state, in open meeting, why I did so. though it grieves me to tell it just as it was.

I very soon found that this conductor was working *his* specialty far beyond the limits utilized by either actors or preachers, or what not ; and this is how he did it. He not only made his little pets do service to show to the best advantage his own attainments, but he strove to heighten this effect by making the same a means for humbling and belittling the real powers and abilities of the group of well-meaning people he was performing before.

And that "riled" me, and made me look further in the same direction. And I say plainly that I have found this transgression much more common than it ought to be, especially among as good a set of men and women as institute conductors generally are.

Why, the other day I came across a case of this kind that, if it had gone a little further, would have been a legitimate field for the exercise of the functions of that officer of the law whose business it is to prevent cruelty to animals.

The "conductor" was doing one of his "specialty acts" in great form, it being, surely, his thousandth performance; and, having concluded, he called on an unsophisticated country girl, who had been doing her level best with her first school for three months, and was still greatly worried as to which was ahead, herself or the "big scholar"—he called on her to "duplicate the bill," as it were! And when she, poor thing, arose and made a stagger at it, he so quizzed, and twitted her, and snubbed her generally, all along the line, that she finally gave up in despair; and, burying her rather fat and shame-flushed face in her hands, she sat down and cried.

Honestly, I almost wondered that the chivalrous, stout fellows who sat on the other side of the room and saw it all, did'nt put the perpetrator of the deed out of doors.

I grant (thank heaven I can honestly do so) that this case was an extreme one, but it was one of the things I saw in my "walks abroad," and I set it down *seriatim, verbatim, in statu quo.* I remark, though, that from my observations I find that cases approaching this one in unpleasantness are not anywhere near as infrequent as they should be in this free and independent land of ours. They should be less frequent still. As Mr. Shakespeare says, "reform it altogether."

Because, the truth is, when you come to look close, a "specialty act" is not the cleverest thing in the world,

after all, either for the performer or the spectator. So far
as the former is concerned, if long indulged in, it tends to
paralyze the nerve of fresh and original thought and
endeavor, and so gradually debilitates its victim. And
for the latter, it is apt to discourage him, especially when
his own crude efforts are brought into strong contrast with
the finished performance of a cunning, not to say crafty,
expert.

Above all, the snobbishness of the fad should be
lopped off, for, truly, there aren't any " av uz all," as
Father Tom would say, who have so very much to boast
of by way of attainment, specialties and all; and even
what we have is very soon learned by those who see us,
day after day !

Which puts me in mind of the remark of an Irish
friend of mine. He used to be very fond of hearing the
Bishop preach, and always went to service when that dig-
nitary held forth. I met him on the street the other
Sunday, though, when I knew the Bishop was preaching,
and asked him why he wasn't in his pew ? To which he
replied :

"Troth, I don't go to hear the Bishop ony more."

"Why! what's the matter ?" I said. " You haven't
gone back on a good man have you ?"

"No," he answered, "but it's the truth I'm tellin'
you, when you've heard the Bishop a half-dozen times *all
after that is variations !* "

"EXAMS."

Speaking of "variations," and of the fact that, after all, there are few men who have such an extended repertoire that they can always favor their audience with a new tune; while, for the most part, the great bulk of mankind have only one or two songs apiece, which are all that nature ever pitched their voices to sing, and which they have to sing over and over again, if they sing at all — I say, all this reminds me that it is one of the most difficult things in the world to size a man up and determine how much there really is in him, by any ordinary tests of measurements that one can arbitrarily bring to bear upon him.

This is especially true if the measurer insists on using his own particular yardstick (which, ten chances to one, is only his own particular "rule of thumb") upon every victim that he would fain take the dimensions of.

My reason for making this observation just here is, that I came across a book the other day which is only "one more of the same sort" that needs to be "called down," if I may use a stage term in these classic pages.

The book is called a "Volume" (why not a volley?) "of Test Questions," and its special mission is set forth in its preface, which declares that it is "designed to fill a long felt want (what a blessing to preface writers a long felt want is) among teachers who are preparing to pass an examination for a State Certificate."

Now here is richness, as Squeers would say. I open the "volume" to find it filled, page after page, with ten thousand (the author assures me on the title page that there are ten thousand, and I take his word for it without stopping to count) disjointed conundrums, with answers attached. The great bulk of the "questions" will perhaps average a short line apiece; and many of the "answers" are equally brief; and together they cover about all that has happened since the pre-historic man sat chattering in his cave, gnawing the bones of his slain adversary.

(Those old ancestors of ours were not without resources for happiness, were they?)

Others of the answers are longer, to be sure, and many of this class are as unsatisfactory as they are extended. This is not the fault of the answers, however, but of the questions that give rise to them. These are so wide-extended that, in many cases, whole volumes have already been written in answer to them without so much as straightening out a single crook of the interrogation marks that forever stand just where these "posers" leave off!

And yet this volume disposes of such questions in a paragraph, and with as much positiveness as though it were giving the date of the last expiring breath of some never-before-heard-of sutler, who perished miserably, while foraging with a company of filibusters in a little 7 by 9 island of the Polynesian group — for it must be understood that this "volume" is especially strong in its expiring-breath department!

Here, then, are a few of the questions that are answered so glibly in the pages before me, but which would be as much unanswered as ever, for me, should I go into a school-room to teach to-morrow morning!

"How is æsthetical culture *best* secured? what its value?

"To what was Arnold's success as a teacher due?" Aye, truly, to what?

"How develop grace, strength, and beauty in pupils?" If we only could!

"How can contrary pupils be managed?" Yea, verily, how can they? There are teachers who can *do* it, but I never saw one who could *tell* me, or anybody else, *how* he did it, so that I or anybody else could do it as he did.

But this book tells!

I wonder if, in a state examination, the candidate should write this answer out, just as it is on the page before me, he would be marked 10 on that point!

"How secure good, and avoid the evil, of praise and blame?" I quote verbatim. Surely the only answer that *could* be given to this question is the one printed in the book; but I am pained to say that even this is less clear than the question that preceeds it!

"What is the use of questions and answers?" Hear! Hear!

"How can the curiosity of children be satisfied?" Honest! that question is in this book, *and there is a printed answer attached!* Need anything more be said? *Can* anything more be said?

And then I find such quantities of unusual and out-of-the-way questions strewn all through the pages, as:

"What is Swedenborgianism?"

"What principles are taught in 'Levana?'"

"What did Milton say about boys?"

Thus far I have failed to find in the interrogatories "Who struck Pat Murphy?" and "Where did McGinty go down into the sea?" but I shall write the author and ask him to embody these important questions in the next edition.

Now, does it seem possible that such questions as these should be set down as the stuff wherewithal to gorge one's self preparatory to an examination for anything, anywhere, to say nothing of an examination regarding one's ability to teach school?

And yet, here is the book before me, and the reader is assure that if he will *memorize these questions and answers* — I suppose the whole 10,000 — he will then be "prepared" to go before the Board of Examiners and successfully compete for that much coveted bit of paper, a State Certificate!

Shades of Mnemosyne, where is Loisette!

Still this book is not so very much worse than others of its kind, or than a good many people who have to examine candidates for certificates, and for college and what not. It is so easy, and such a temptation to ask, unusual or unanswerable, questions! I wonder if there isn't some special faculty of meanness in us all that makes us like to "knock out," so to speak, almost anybody whom we get where we can question him at will?

Speaking of this, a friend of mine, who had recently passed an examination, said, in view of the unusual and irrelevant questions that were asked him, "I should like to turn the tables on my examiner and ask him questions for awhile!"

"And what would you have asked him?" I said.

"Oh, I'd have given him some easy ones — questions that quantities of boys ten years old can answer, but which would have been posers to him."

"For instance?" I said.

"Well," he replied, "How would these do for starters:"

"What is blacklash, and how would you take it up?"

"How would you upset a key?"

" Define template and contemplate, and show the difference between them!"

"What is the meaning of f. o. b.; 30, 3 off 10?"

Somehow I secretly wished that he could have taken a turn-about with his interrogator, and if he could have kept it up, as above, I should like to lay two to one in his favor.

And yet I find, upon looking up the answers to these questions, that they are not so very unusual after all. The third one is slightly tricky, but I've seen scores that were more so, on "really truly" examination lists.

And this brings me back to my starting point, namely, that it is a very difficult thing to size a man up, and fairly determine what there is in him, by any arbitrary methods that can be brought to bear upon him. The only way I know of, that amounts to anything, is to see him *actually at work* in the field, or calling, he claims to be fitted to labor in.

And here is where it seems to me, "the children of this world are wiser than the children of light," counting teachers as "the parties of the second part" in the above combination.

For, if one goes to a bank, or a mill, or a store, and asks for a position, there isn't a banker, or a master mechanic, or a merchant, who would ever think of giving the applicant a written examination on odds and ends "from Adam down," to test his efficiency.

Examined, the person would surely be, but the questions would be few and pointed. "What experience have you had in a position similar to the one you seek?" would cover nearly all the ground outside the question of character.

And is not this good common sense, and would it not work as well in determining the fitness of teachers as of book-keepers, mechanics and clerks? Let any expert teacher talk with a candidate for fifteen minutes, and he can tell his fitness to teach far better than as though he should ask, and the fellow should answer all the 10,000 questions in the book before me.

Indeed, there *are* men who might be able to answer *all* these ten thousand questions, and yet who could not teach a country school successfully.

All of which means that *the ability to answer questions is but a very slight indication of one's ability to teach school.*

And as for state examinations, and the issuing of state certificates, why should not this be put into the hands of a state Board of Examiners, whose business it should be to visit, personally, the applicant, and see him with his every-day clothes on, at work in his own school-room? This would be a test direct, pointed, vital. It would mean a thousand fold more than any document can possibly mean under present methods, for it would have a personality behind it that would be of untold power.

Why! I would a hundred times rather "try for a state certificate" by having a committee sit in personal judgment on my work as a teacher, than by filling myself up with any "ten thousand test questions" that ever were made, and seeing how many of them I could carry to the examination table without spilling; and there, in solemn silence, unload a few of them upon foolscap (good name that) as a voucher for my ability as a teacher!

And heaven knows I should stand a better show for getting what I sought by the first method than by the last. For, with due modesty let me say that I consider it not impossible that I might acquire the art of teaching school so as to win the approval of those who were capable of judging what creditable teaching is; but to answer, on foolscap, the questions that are now given to a candidate for a state certificate - I couldn't do it to save my life.

And what is more, I couldn't learn to do it. It isn't in me.

And yet the fault is not in my ability *to teach*. It has nothing whatever to do with that. The trouble lies in another quarter, namely, in my *memory*. I haven't the *memory for detail* that one must have who successfully passes the examinations for the highest honors among teachers.

And what is true in my case is just as true of many men and women who have been successfully teaching for years. We all know these people. They are among the best teachers to be found anywhere, and there is not the shadow of a doubt as to their ability to fill, with credit to themselves and benefit to their patrons, any position in our public schools.

And yet these teachers cannot hold a state certificate to this effect, because, forsooth, they have not the ability to cram their memories with dry details and disgorge them on call.

And right here lies the chief offense of all, namely, that our present method of examination for this high honor is on a wrong basis, in that it is, *almost entirely*, a *memory test, while the possession of mnemonic ability is no proof whatever of one's real merit as a school teacher.*

Surely these things ought not longer so to be in a nation that stands so well toward the front of the educational line as does the United States.

I have not space to go into the details of the working of such a method as I have hinted at, nor is there need that I do so; for I know the educational fraternity of this country well enough to know that they can work such a plan out to a successful issue, if once they undertake to do it; and in justice to themselves they ought to labor to

make the test of the highest ability in their ranks of a
kind that would really measure such ability, and not let it
remain what it is now — a mere trial of the strength of a
faculty that has next to nothing to do with real worth in
the school room.

Why not have this issue raised at the National
Teachers' Association, and thoroughly discussed by that
honorable body? Anyhow, something ought to be done
about it, for it is a live issue, and one that is of vital interest to every genuine teacher in our beloved common-
wealth.

Such a plan might work sad havoc with ten-thousand-
test-question volumes, and their like, but the winds would
blow, and the world roll around, even if these should be
thrown into the waste basket, where they really belong.

RATS.

"Now, chentlemen, efery man must make a liefin'
some vay, und I makes mine by rats!   I don't got so werry
rich by it, but I chenerally manage to got along butty
vell.   Der vay I makes it, I gives a rat show; und I don't
sharge any man a cent to see it; but ven he sees it, off he
likes it, he can gif my rats vat he bleases, und ve vill gone
about our beezness.

"Now, off you stands a leedle pack, chentlemen —
poys, got back on der sidevalk ! — I show you vot I got
in dis pox."

He was a grimy-faced Bohemian, and while he was
making the little speech just quoted, he stood in the open
street, a few feet from the curbstone, and immediately in

front of the postoffice, to which the people were flocking for their morning mail.

While he spoke, a crowd of curious men and boys gathered about, and by the time he had finished his opening remarks they were beginning to press in upon him quite closely. He waved them back to the sidewalk, and then proceeded to make ready for his performance.

He first spread out a tripod which stood about shoulder high, and on this placed an oblong box which was about two feet long, one foot wide and perhaps nine inches high. From one end of this box he rigged an extension in the shape of a platform about four feet long and a foot wide. This was the stage upon which his actors were presently to appear, and on which their performance was to be given.

Having completed these arrangements, he opened the end of the box which was nearest the platform. Instantly there was a rush from within, and a dozen or more of rats poured themselves out on the narrow stage. They were of all ages and sizes, some gray and some white, but all —rats. They scurried along the board and climbed over the box, sniffing the air, and now and then stopping to gaze at the crowd.

Presently some of them began to climb over the edge of the box and to let themselves down to the ground by means of the legs of the tripod. Once on *terra firma*, they scampered over the paving stones and ran toward the people standing about, who immediately began to retreat. Then the master of ceremonies spoke again, this time addressing the rats:

"Ha! ha! take care dere! Don't schare der beople's! Come! Come!" And at this request the rats ran back to where their master stood and formed in a circle all about him. Then he again addressed the crowd:

"Nein! Nein! goot beoples, dose rats vouldn't hurt nopody. I deach dem better manners as dat. See!"

He lifted his hands, and at the sign the rats began to clamber up his legs. They ran all over him. Some crawled into his pockets and presently came forth again with bits of bread or cheese that they had found there. Some ran under his coat and came creeping out from beneath his coat collar. He took first one and then another in his hand, talking to them and the crowd alternately, always in an easy, good natured way that seemed to please both his two-legged and his four-legged hearers.

"Und now ve vill gif der beople's a leedle show, eh! Come, Blondin, und let me see off you can valk dot tight rope across Niagara yet!"

He had stretched a line from a pole at the further end of the little platform to a similar one at the further end of the box. The distance was about six feet, and the line was as large as your finger.

Then the rat called Blondin, climbed up one of the poles and mounted the rope. He cautiously crept across it from end to end, having done which he ran down the other pole to the platform, sniffed toward the crowd and then ambled away into the box, much as a pretty "elocutionist reader" would smile, and make a little bow, and then trot off into the wings of the stage after she had made a hit with the house and while the clapping of hands was at its height!

This was the "opening," and after it there followed much more that was quite as clever. The rats marched across the platform in single file, and by twos and fours, even as we have seen the Knights of this or that parade themselves on Saint somebody's day. One fired a pistol and another rang a bell, while the third turned a crank of a small music box. It was a good show, and well worth

the pennies, nickels and dimes that were presently sought
from the crowd in a novel way, as the master of ceremonies said:

"Now, chentlemen, you haf see vot my rats can done,
und I dink you vill gif dem rats someding to vill der
stomachs mit, eh? And vat you vill gif, yoost drow it on
der ground, und dose rats vill dake care of it, eh! poys?"

Some one threw a nickel into the street, and immediately one of the rats galloped away and picked it up
with his mouth, while others of the lot sniffed toward the
crowd, their little eyes glittering as they watched for a
duplicate of the money-throwing performance. It was
great sport, and for several minutes there was a generous
shower of small coins which the rats took care of as fast
as they fell. They brought all the money to the master,
who did "impetticose the gratility" after a manner which
was worthy of Touchstone himself.

Finally everybody seemed to have enough for that
time — crowd, rats, master and all — and the show was
over. The rats returned to their box, one and all, and
were shut into it; the platform was taken down, the tripod
folded up, and each went his way.

I was always fond of curious shows, and I stood this
one through to the end with great satisfaction. When it
was all over, and the proprietor had folded his traps and
was silently stealing away, I followed him for a little distance to see what next.

For I hardly knew which to marvel at most, the man
or his beasts; and it seemed to me that who could do so
much could also do much more, and I wanted to see it all.

The fellow went a little ways up-town, and then
turned off on a by-street, where he drew up under the
shade of a large tree, set his box on the ground, seated

himself beside it and began feeding his performers. The boys followed him, and we all stood about watching.

"Presently my soul grew stronger," as did Mr. Poe's when he had a raven instead of a rat to make him fearsome, and I ventured to address a remark to the manager of the combination, as follows:

"How long have you been in this business, sir?"

And to me he replied: "Not so werry long mit rats; but always I can do vot I likes mit animals of all ginds! I vas a long dime mit horses und dogs, but apout fife years ago I try rats, und I likes it pedder."

"Where do you get your rats?" I asked.

"Oh, efery blace I go," he answered. "I don't keep a rat so werry long, so I haf to got new vones all de dime."

"Why can't you keep them?" I asked. "Do they run away?'

"Oh, no!" he replied. "My rats nefer runs avay! But I vorks my rats puddy hardt, und der box don't bin so werry big, und — oh, vell, *nodding liffs so werry long off you dook dem avay from vere dey pelongs!*"

"How long will a rat live?" said I.

"Dot derpends on ver he is, und off he don't get caught! Now, off a rat has a goot korn grib to liff in, und don't get caught, he liffs — oh, vel, fife, seex, ten years! But its a puddy goot rat as lasdst me seex mondh."

"How long does it take you to teach them their tricks?" I queried.

"Oh, vell, I couldn't tole you dat ogzackly. *It derpends on der rat!* Now off I got a goot, bright rat, I deach him to do vot he vill learn in two, dree days. But off I got a rat is a tam fool (this man was a worldling, and he spoke the vernacular), vell, I could nefer teach him nodding!"

"But," I said, "if a rat is bright can you teach him anything you choose?"

"Oh, no!" he replied. "*Some rats vill learn some dings, und some udder rats vill learn some udder dings.* Und dots a funny ding apout dat! *You can't always dell py der looks of a rat yoost vot he vill learn!*" and as he said this he spoke to a rat that was gnawing a bone:

"Cheneral Grant, come here!"

The rat addressed caught up the bone and dragged it over to where the man sat, who then continued, as he picked the rodent up and stroked him with his hand:

"Now, I galls dis rat Cheneral Grant pecause he shoots der gun. I try more as feefty rats pefore I gets von dot vill shoot a gun. Und ven I gets dis veller, I tries to make him valk der rope. Der Blondin vot I got dot dime, he vas got his leg broke, und I vants a rat to took his blace. But I don't could make him valk a rope von leedle bit. *It vos not in him to do someding like dot!*"

"Vel, den I try him mit der gun, und py chiminy he make him go right avay! He likes it! He vill shoot all der dime off I let him! Eh, Cheneral!" And he chucked the rat under the chin as it jumped off his hand and returned to its bone again.

Just at this moment a great lubberly rat came rolling up towards the "Cheneral." He seized his military brother by the scruff of the neck, and with an easy toss sent him spinning through the air, the bone falling to the lot of the bulldozer in the fray. But the master came to the rescue, and with a smart rap he made the victor give up his spoil, while he went on, a little excitedly, to explain :

"Now, dot rat," indicating the big one he had just called to order, "I calls John L. Sullifan! He don't know nodding but viting, und you don't nefer could deach him nodding else! *I don't pelieve Got Almighdy could effer deach dot rat nodding but viting! But he can vight!* Py chiminy! he licks any udder rat I effer see! Dot's vy I geeps him! Some dimes some vellers dey likes to have a rat-vight. I don't myself like it so werry much, but I chust geeps John L. Sullifan for dem fellers, und he can vip all de rats dey can pring him. Dot's all he vos goot for!"

We all laughed, and he continued : "But all rats don't been dot vay. Patti! Patti!" he called.

A plump little, fine-haired rat responded to his call, and, leaving the group, climbed into his hand, while he said : "Dot's der rat vot blays der moosic-box. Und she like it, too, eh, Patti?"

The little creature stood on its hind legs as he spoke, and began moving one of its fore-paws round and round, as if turning a crank, while her master went on :

" Eh, you see, she vant to tole me to got der moosic-pox. No, no! not now, leedle gal. Go ead your preak-fast now, und ven ve gif anodder show, den you blays again."

He put her on the ground, and she ran away into the crowd of her brethren and sisters.

"And so," I said, "I understand that you can't teach *any* rat to do anything you happen to want him to learn to do?"

"Oh, nein, nein!" he replied. " *You can't only deach a rat to do vot he vos made to do!* Und ven a man is a goot rat-deacher, he knows dot ding, und *he von't dry to deach a rat vot he can't learn!*"

" *Und dot is yoost der tifference between a goot rat-deacher und a shool-deacher!*" he added. "A shool-deacher, he dinks he can deach any shild anyding vot he bleases. But he couldn't do id! *Shildren is yoost like rats! Some vill learn von ding, und some vill learn anoder ding, und dot's a goot shool-deacher dot knows dot ding, und vorks dot vay !"*

"Do you suppose *I* could ever learn to teach rats as you do ?" I faltered.

The man eyed me a moment, and then said : "No ! you couldn't do it ! You vasn't der right kint off a man ! *Ven a man makes a goot rat-deacher he vos got to been born yoost on burpose for dot beezness, und I don't peleef you vos born dot vay !"*

The boys laughed, and I think they had a right to. Then we all went away.

It was an old Roman who said, *Poeta nascitur non fit.* A modern American has said : "Culture can increase the size, quality and flavor, but it cannot change the kind !"

When will our public school managers learn the lesson and act accordingly ?

"DOT."

I have a friend who often says to me when we meet, "If you've got anything good about you, pass it around!" I happen to have something good about me to-day, and most gladly do I proceed to share it.

This something is in the shape of a letter. It was never meant for the public eye, and so you will please consider it as strictly *inter nos.* The man who wrote it is the most modest man I ever knew, but the story he tells is *so* good that I have finally persuaded him to let *you* read what he wrote just to *me*, as follows. He says:

"This is the first leisure moment I have had since we got back, and I will improve it by telling you something of our trip. We hoped to see you on our way home, but the train was away late, and we hardly expected you to sit up for us. However, late as we were, the conductor on the other road knew we were coming, and *he held his train for us forty minutes.*

And that is only a sample of the kind of treatment we received all along the way. Everywhere, going and coming, and at the Capitol, people seemed to vie with each other in trying to minister to the enjoyment of the clean, bright-looking set of young people I had with me.

"I remember that you once said, when you were here, that I ought to be a proud man among my school children, and I can tell you, without boasting, that my heart swelled not a little (*perhaps* my head, too) at the many compliments upon the appearance and behavior of the pupils, from the strangers with whom we came in contact.

"There were an even fifty of us — all my high school pupils — who left here Thursday morning at 3 o'clock, and we got back at about the same hour on Saturday morning. Of course, the children were pretty tired when we got home, but '*Dot*' was along and had mothered them all so carefully that, after a good sleep, they every one came up as well as ever."

(I take my hat off, here, ladies and gentlemen, and reverently explain that "Dot" is the little woman who sits at the table opposite the good man who wrote this letter. Her true name is Rebecca, but she never grew quite tall enough to match the ideal in person, either of the stately Hebrew woman who lighted off her camel to meet Isaac in the field, or that other Rebecca whom Sir Walter has made famous; so her husband just calls her "Dot," and that tells the whole story.

I should like to stop right here, though, and say a word or two about her.

She is a born mother, and one who has never had to adopt lap dogs to fill the places at her table! She has borne six children. Four of these yet remain to call her blessed, and two have "gone before." But there is mother enough in her, you will observe, to meet the felt wants of fifty boys and girls who are off on a two-day's outing.

She is a very quiet little woman. You would hardly

notice her among a crowd of grand ladies, and I never heard of her being president of anything; but she is a queen in her own home, and that is what counts, according to my way of thinking. Those fifty children think so, too, and that is what counts in the town where her husband is teaching!

But I started out to let the letter tell the story.)

"You want to know what we had planned for the trip and how it panned out.

"Well, in the first place, the plan was very simple. While I was at the capitol, during the holidays, it occurred to me what an education it would be for our boys and girls to see that truly fine building, with its elegantly finished halls and offices; its historical and symbolical paintings and reliefs and statuary; how much of reality it would put into their history study and into their every-day reading, if they could see our various state officers at work in their offices; and above all, to see the legislature in regular session, carrying on its actual work of law-making.

"Then there were the museums, and the libraries, and the grand stairway, and the magnificent building itself.

"Besides this, we had planned only for a visit to the Lincoln Monument and the Lincoln homestead. There was enough, however, it seemed to me, for a two-day's jaunt, and I kept thinking and thinking how much the children would enjoy it and how much good it would do them.

"Well, somehow the idea stuck to me, and when I got home I wrote to the agent of the railroad for rates. The first reply was discouraging, for it would have made the cost of the round trip, hotel fare and all, about $6.50 each. This was too much, for where there were two or three from a family, or, in some cases if only one, the cost would have shut out the very ones I wanted most should be benefited by the plan.

"Here was one of the times when I wished I were rich enough to just put my hand down in my pocket and haul out enough to pay the children's way; but I couldn't, and there was no use fretting.

Yet the idea had taken such a hold on me that I couldn't drop it. I stated the case to some of our good people, and told them that the whole expense would be somewhere about $250. Almost to my surprise one after another said ' I'll put in $10,' and ' I will,' and ' I will,' until, in one afternoon I had the first hundred dollars in sight.

" It took a good deal of walking and talking to get it all, but I got it, and the children have had their trip *and there is nearly a dollar left!*

" After a good deal of correspondence, I succeeded in getting the railroad fare reduced so that the whole cost, *per capita*, for railroad fare, hotel fare, street car fare, and admission to Lincoln's Monument, altogether, was only $5.19. After a good deal of enjoyment in anticipation, we started, made the whole trip in safety, delivered the young folks to their parents, and checked them off.

" Thus ended my responsibility for them.

" How did it pan out? Well, in the first place, I suppose it would have been impossible to chock any more solid enjoyment into those two days of the children's lives with anything less than a ten-ton pile driver. They just enjoyed every minute of it, and so did I. Nor has there been any reaction. I never saw them better natured and more studious than they are this week.

" That isn't all; we know each other bettter. and I am, as I said, prouder of them than ever before. Then, too, some little traits cropped out here and there, that I shall keep in mind and deal with in a sort of fatherly way when the proper opportunities come, from time to time!

" We were fortunate in striking a very interesting session of the House. An important bill was coming up. The children saw the dallying over the reading of the journal as we afterwards learned to kill time and pass the introduction of the bill over into the next week.

" After a number of bills had been introduced and referred to their appropriate committees, we got a glimpse of a little political fine work. The bill in question was supposed to be in the hands of a man whose name was way down in the R's, and the opponents of it expected to adjourn the session long before his name could be reached in the call. But during the morning the bill was put in charge of a Mr. Fowler—up in the F's you see—who plumped the bill in upon the astonished House, and asked unanimous consent to have it passed to first reading without going to a committee.

" Objection being made, he, without yielding the floor, moved a suspension of the rules to the same purpose.

After some sparring, the vote was taken, the rules suspended, and the bill read for the first time and placed on the calendar for second reading. Since our return we are all alive and on the look out to watch the fate of that bill. We all have a personal interest in it now, and shall watch it to its final fate.

"I speak of this so minutely, because it shows, better than I can tell in any other way, how the 'Idea' of the trip was realized. I did not ask the children to carry note books and use their pencils; *I just let them go and use their eyes and their ears.* This they did, and I am satisfied. They show it by their talk.

"Of course there were ever so many things connected with the trip that I should like to tell you of, but I haven't time to write them out, here and now. I only add that, on the way down, the route agent took the boys and girls, in small squads, into the mail car and let them see how mail is 'thrown.'

"Then, for the evening that we were in the city, I arranged with some friends of mine who live there to entertain the young people at their home. This they did in elegant style, and it was a most excellent experience for the boys and girls.

"Besides this there was the ride there and back, the country and cities we passed through, the jostling against people which all this necessitated, and, by far from being least of all, the stay at the hotel, and the ordering for the first time for many of them, of a meal from a bill of fare.

"Very simple things, all these, to be sure, but I cannot help believing that the experiences of these two days have done more than months of mere school-going could do toward fitting these children to take a hold on the life they are destined to live. I counted that the trip would put new life and meaning into their studies and all their school work when they got home again, and I am certain that it has done all that and more too.

"To be sure, if I had to lead out my flock again I see many places where I could improve the management of such a trip. Who couldn't? And yet, take it all in all, I am pretty well satisfied, and so are the children, and so are their parents and friends who furnished the wherewithal for the outing. What more could I ask?"

There, that is the letter, and it struck me as one of the best things I have seen or known about for many a day.

Of course there is nothing so very *great* about it all —

7

that is, great when measured by a world-wide-renown tape line ; but the longer I live the better I know that it is not what makes "all the world wonder" that is of value to you and to me.

You see, there are so many folks in the world ; and, take them altogether, they care so little for things — for what you and I do, any how.

I am never so lonesome as when I am in a big city, where there are thousands and thousands of people all about me, not one of whom I know, not one who knows or cares for me.

I am sure that the next edition of the " History of the World, from the Beginning to the Present Time," will make no mention of the incident which the above-quoted letter describes. But, for all that, I would rather have such a chapter as this written in my Book of Life than to have pages and pages devoted to me in any World's History that ever went to press.

Perhaps I get this feeling from what I read *between the lines* of this letter, and which I am sure is there for any one to read who has eyes to see what there really is on the pages before me.

That little touch about " Dot's being along," concerning which I have already remarked (and you must remember that this letter was not penned in any studied way — it was never written for effect. I have quoted it just as it came to me, fresh from the warm and enthusiastic heart of the man who wrote it, and who never dreamed, when writing it, that *you* would ever see it — that would have spoiled all.)

How many pages do you think it would take to tell *all* that is said in those three words, " Dot was along ? "

Put over against them the description even of a great inauguration ball, and see if those three little words do not mean more to *you* than all the columns of description about that magnificent affair? I have nothing to say against the ball. It was all right, in its place. But I read in the paper for that day an incident connected with the inauguration in Washington which means more to me (and I believe to all the people in this country, as well) than all else that took place on that great occasion.

And this is what I read: "Just before the President left the White House to go to the Capitol to take the oath of office, after he had said *au revoir* to the company of notable personages who had assembled to see him off, his wife called him back for a moment, and, throwing her arms around his neck, kissed him (even if all the people did see), and, with happy and hopeful tears in her eyes said, 'God bless you, my husband, and Godspeed.'"

And I am here to state that if the president is the man I take him to be, he prizes that loving tribute from his wife more than all the honors that were showered upon him during the entire inauguration ceremonies and festivities. Give us a nation full of wives and mothers like "Dot" and the mistress of the White House (and they are of the same quality, though one lives in state and the other is only a teacher's wife), and we will weather through, and successfully settle the silver question, and the tariff issue, and all the other ills that may rise up to trouble this great nation of ours.

If only "Dot is along" it will come out all right, somehow, and I know it.

And then there is that quiet little passage: "Besides this, we know each other better than we did before; and then, too, some little traits have cropped out, here and there, that I shall keep in mind and deal with in a sort of fatherly way, when proper opportunities come, from time to time!"

How many pages more would it take to write out all that is between *those* lines ?

Truly, happy is that teacher that can do the like of this, and happy is that pupil who has a teacher that can deal with him in a fatherly way as opportunities offer !

What wonder that Mr. Emerson told his daughter that he didn't care *what* she studied, but that he *did* care with whom she studied !

And, for my part, I would a thousand times rather have a child of mine be the pupil of a teacher who could and would " deal with him in a *fatherly way* " than to have him sit at the feet of the most learned LL.D., A. M., B. A., F. R. S., and all the rest of the alphabet, that ever set spectacles astride an emaciated nose, and grew dry and sandy from digging in the graves of dead ages, but who lacked this *one* thing.

And then to have some one break the ice for you when, *for the first time,* you go to a hotel and are brought face to face with a printed bill of fare ! As the old hymn says, " O, what eternal horrors hang around " that bill of fare, under such circumstances ! Don't *I* remember, and don't *you* remember what a time *we* had with it ?

It was at the Waddell House, Cleveland, Ohio, that it first happened to me. I was seventeen, and was away from home alone for the first time.

I got up at five o'clock in the morning, and was mad because breakfast wasn't ready ! And I said so, too — told the proprietor (night clerk) that I had my opinion of a house that would charge a man (?) $3.00 a day, and make him wait around for an hour for breakfast !

And at six, when the big dining-room door swung open, I went into breakfast all alone ! Not a soul else to sit down to those two acres of tables and dishes but myself !

And when a red-headed waiter-girl, in a much-bestarched calico gown which rattled like stage thunder as she bore down on me, thrust that bill of fare under my nose — O, I can't go on and tell it all! It is more than thirty years since it happened, yet it gives me the horrors, even now, just to write about it.

And to be saved all this. To have "Dot along" to show a fellow how — as Mr. Gounod says in his opera, " Oh, bliss ! oh, rapture !"

But the chief thing about it all, to me, is, that this teacher got an *idea of his own*, and without consulting Pestalozzi, or Froebel, or any other "authority," he had the head and the heart to carry that idea to a successful issue.

Not that *you*, or anybody else, should try to do just what he did. Not that! If you, teaching in a small town, as this man is, or in a large town either, for that matter, should try to do *just* what he did, you would probably fail at it.

But if you can get an *idea* that, worked out, you think will be of value to your children ; and if you get that idea so hard that it "sticks to you," and you can not and will not let it alone until you can say : " I have done what I planned and I am pretty well satisfied with the result, and so are those for whom I planned and wrought " — if you can do this, then you may know, to a certainty, that you are among the elect in the fraternity ; that your " call to teach " was a genuine voice from heaven, and not some other noise that you heard, but didn't understand.

THE BAD BOY'S MOTHER.

It is a great comfort to me, in my "walks abroad," to know that I am not traveling alone, but have companions by the way, friends who chat with me as I go along, and who call my attention to this or that object of interest or importance, which I should, perhaps, miss altogether if they did not point it out to me.

Indeed, this is the greatest thing in life, this companionship by the way. Take that out, and there would be very little left in this world worth living for. It is sympathy that we all crave ; and if there be any human blood in us, we are heart-sick and discouraged if we do not get what we so much long for.

Oh, I know what the poets say concerning solitude, and all that, and I am well aware that there is a kind of truth in what they are trying to get at ; nevertheless, I am heartily in accord with Dundreary, when he says that " of course birds of a feather flock together, for nothing but a very idiot of a bird would go off and try to flock all alone by its own self!"

And Walt Whitman is equally correct when he says, " Whoever walks a furlong without sympathy, marches at his own funeral dressed in his shroud!"

And that is the reason why this batch of letters before me is worth while — letters that have been written to me by my fellow-travelers in my " walks abroad " — for every scrap of paper in the bunch contains some word from a companion, some " See here," or " Don't you think ?" or " Have you ever noticed ?" or " It seems to me," or something of that sort.

For instance, the letter on the top of the pile is written in a feminine hand — a good, trim, tailor-made-suit sort of a hand — and it says to me :

"The evolution of the bad boy of the school is a problem that taxes my resources to the utmost, and when there is added to this the *involution* of the bad boy's mother, what is flesh and blood to do ?"

The interrogation mark which stands at the end of this sentence in the letter is as large and as grappling in appearance as the iron hook at the end of an old-fashioned log chain. All of which I interpret to mean, "Answer that, sir, so as to settle the business once for all, and you shall have the biggest medal that the World's Fair can possibly stamp out and mold up."

"Well," as the preachers say when tackling a mighty theme (and surely the bad boy's mother may justly be considered a mighty almost anything), "I should make a distinction." That is, it would make all the difference in the world to me what kind of a woman the bad boy's mother was, as to how I should treat her.

If she were a stupid female, who felt that something was wrong, she hardly knew what, and whose boy had worried the life out of her till she hardly knew whether she were dead or alive — why, in such case, I should do my best to be patient and keep still, and let the poor creature unburden her mind. It does such a woman a great deal of good just to talk, and if I could busy myself at correcting papers, or making out averages, or going through some of the other rigmarole and red-tape motions that the system subjects me to, while she told her story, or abused me, as the case might be, I should count myself happy.

And, if she were an arrogant person, rich and mean, I

should be inclined to treat her in something of the same fashion, only being more blasè than ever in her case.

Indeed, it is held by many of the great teachers of this glorious land of ours that the "keep-still" method of treating these fearsome females works better than anything else that they have ever tried.   It is an exceedingly wearying thing, they claim, to beat the air ; and many a prize-fighter has been eventually "knocked out" by an antagonist who was no where near as hard a hitter as himself, but who knew enough to keep out of the way till the giant was winded, and who then got in his work.

And so, in general, the answer on this line would be, keep out of the bad boy's mother's way when she takes a hand in the game.   Say nothing to her.   Let her talk till she is tired, and if she gives out, ask her if she hasn't something more on her mind !

In a word, shake the red rag of your own silence in her face, and dodge her by bending more closely than ever over whatever you are ostensibly working at when she "charges," and ten chances to one she will break down and cry inside of five minutes ; and when she does that, she is yours to escort to the door !

To be sure, such a method seems to me to be abominably mean, but there is an old maxim that says something about fighting the devil with fire, and the above comes as near that as it is possible to attain in these premises.   So I note it as *one* of the things that might be done when you have a case of the "involution of the bad boy's mother," and it is a way that *works*, as many a teacher can testify.

However, this is only what "flesh and blood" would do, and I have mentioned it because that is what my walking companion asked advice about.

As to what the *spirit* would do, that is another question.

And it is the spirit that ought to handle these cases, and which is fully capable of doing so without any advice from me or anybody else. Keep the flesh and blood of yourself in the background, your spirit holding it by the collar, as if it were an angry dog bristling for a fight (and that is what it is, for the most part), and let your soul come to the front and take control of things, and your troubles on this count will be well nigh ended ere they are fairly begun.

It was a wise man who said, "A soft answer turneth away wrath, but grievous words stir up strife."

And do not forget that, in many cases (my experience is in a majority of cases), the bad boy's mother has a side to her suit that you can well afford to listen to and consider. It may be hard for you to take a lesson at her hands, but many a teacher has grown exceeding wise on such instruction.

As a rule, the mother knows her boy far better than you do, and a thousand chances to one she has more at stake in him than you possibly can have.

And, besides this, as many schools are now organized, on the ultra-graded plan, the probabilities are not a few that the complaining witness has good grounds for her "involution" in the case.

If her boy is slow in some particular branch of study, and for this cause has been kept back in other studies in which he is bright (and thousands of boys, both good and bad, have been dealt with in this way), and for this reason he has become nettled and aggravated until he has turned bad just to get even with his persecutors — if this is the situation (and I suspect that such is the case much oftener than the average teacher would willingly admit), then, if the mother comes to plead for, or to *demand* equity and justice for her offspring, hear her, I beseech you. She has a right to be heard, and as God lives, she will be heard, some day, whether you listen to her or not.

The school is for her boy, and not her boy for the school, and if things are not this end to she has full cause for "involution" till matters are set right.

But it is useless to extenuate. There is no end to the subject. One could write about it till the crack of doom and still the half would not be told. I think all that can wisely be said about it is, "make a distinction," and be sure, every time, that the mother has everything that can possibly conduce to the best interest and welfare of her bad boy.

INCORRIGIBLES.

Another fellow-traveler writes: "To what extent should the public school be made a reform school? or, in other words, How long should the whole school suffer the presence of a refractory or incorrigible pupil?"

And here again I must beg to reply that I should "make a distinction."

If a pupil is *wholly incorrigible*, I should say that the public school should not be burdened with him for a single moment; just as, if a pupil has the small-pox or the diphtheria, he should at once be removed.

But the question is, *is* the pupil of this sort?

That is an item that should be well considered, and very deliberately acted upon.

My own opinion, based upon my experience, is that a very small percentage of those who are ordinarily counted as bad boys in school are "incorrigible."

I suppose there *are* boys of the *utterly bad sort;* but I say, frankly, that I never yet met one who was wholly that way !

It is with me about this as it has been about meeting
villains such as we see depicted on the stage — the man
who gets a mortgage on the farm, and falls in love with
the sweet daughter, and then turns down the thumb
screws till the girl says yes, and her father falls headlong
into a desperate grave! I have seen all this played a
hundred times, and have often wondered that I have never
met one of these gifted villains in society; but, thus far,
not one of them has crossed my track, so far as I know.
They may have done so, but if they have I have failed to
recognize them.

I have seen a great many *stupid* people who did wrong,
and some very wicked ones who persisted in their evil
doing long after I thought they ought to stop; and I have
even seen some people who thought they were exceedingly good, who have done things that seemed to me not
a little shady. Indeed, if I crowd the case far enough, I
am forced to acknowledge certain acts of my own, that,
according to some plumb lines, might be found some
degrees "out of true;" but, with all this on the wrong side
of the ledger, I am certain that I never met an "incorrigible!" I do not say that there are no such people, I
only insist that, in the distribution of prizes, such a one
has never fallen to my lot.

And yet I know that there are such people, and sometimes they are boys, for I remember the sad and awful
story of Jesse Pomeroy, the boy murderer, of Boston, who
took delight in cutting the throats of little girls, and I
suppose there are similar cases in other towns.

And if I had *such* a boy in school, I firmly believe
that he ought not to remain therein a single day. And
boys (or girls) who are habitual thieves, or vicious, or
licentious, or insane, on any criminal line (for who can
believe otherwise than that all such people are unbalanced

in mind?), all these should be eliminated from the public
school, *but these only.*

The boy who is only mischievous, and who loves fun
better than he loves books, he should not be forced to go.
That is not what the school is for, to turn *him* out.

To be sure he is a burden, but he is a burden to be
borne rather than thrown in the ditch. To dump him is
an easy way out of the trouble, for the time being, but it
is the coward's way, the lazy teacher's way, the shirk's
way, the sneak's way. It is not the way of the teacher
who is called of God to teach, and who believes in himself
as God's minister among the children!

Do you know that the great bulk of what we call
wickedness in this world is really stupidity?

I have a friend who once had a greater strain put upon
his integrity than he was able to stand up under, and the
result was he was forced to spend a year in the peniten-
tiary. He is a bright man, and he kept his eyes wide open
while undergoing this terrible ordeal. He has told me
some of the things he learned while in prison, and the
most impressive thing he has said to me is that more than
nine-tenths of all the convicts who are undergoing penal
servitude are men who are absolutely incapable of taking
care of themselves! They are tramps—dependent, erratic,
cunning, half-made-up fellows, who are far weaker than
they are wicked, and in many cases more stupid than
either.

And I wonder if such is not much the situation
among the alleged bad boys of our schools. And is it
not true, too, that, for the most part, the bad boys that
bother us most are those that have no head for books?
And don't you begin to realize that there are ever so many
people in this world who have no head for books, though
they may have fair, yes, great abilities in other directions?

For instance, there is my gardener, who scarcely ever reads a word, though he had a good fair chance to attend school when a boy. He has no delight in books. I doubt if he ever read a story in his life, and as for taking up Tennyson, or holding his own in a Browning club — you laugh!

But you ought to see the garden this man can make; the roses he can coax into bloom when my friend the learned Professor of Botany has given them up; the radishes he has ready for our table long before any of our neighbors have them, and so on to the further end of the garden.

And the delight he takes in all this is something that it does one's soul good to see.

I did not know him in school, but if I could get at his record there I strongly suspect that his deportment would be much below 100, and that he was counted a bad boy. But I do not believe that he was an "incorrigible." Anyhow, he is far enough from that in his present place, and something pretty severe would have to happen before I should expel him from the position he now holds.

Is there a hint in this for you, my fellow-travelers, or for you who are looking on and seeing what we are saying to each other?

There are a good many things that happen in school that it doesn't pay the teacher to see. Boys will be boys, and girls, girls; and children are not old folks. Thank God they are not, and that they can not be made to be. And as long as they are not malicious and criminal, my notion is that it ought to be a *very* rare thing for one of these little ones to perish out of the public schools. Don't take their shortcomings and capers too seriously. Remember when you oh, but this is wormwood: but that herb makes a healthful, though a bitter draught!

Truly, it is only last week, as we were cleaning house, that the woman who was going to the bottom and top of everything to make all clean, knocked down a little, old spool-box from an upper shelf in a closet, where it had lain, undisturbed, for many and many a year. It fell open as it struck the floor, and out rolled a heap of little notes, all folded small, and written in the daintiest hand. From the looks of the chirography, a very paragon of all the feminine virtues wrote those pages.

And it was a lovely girl who penciled them, and as good as she was lovely. She was very scholarly too. All these notes of hers are written in Latin. She was eighteen at the time, and ought to have been above such doings; and I know that she knew it was against the rules to do as she did. She loved books, and stood at the head of her class. And yet she wrote every one of those notes to me, in school time, looking on her book all the while as though she were studying with all her might; and when she had written them, she folded them up small, even as they all show to this day, and threw them across three rows of seats to where I sat and caught them on the fly!

I do not know where she is now. The last I heard of her she was a matronly school ma'am, teaching in a high school; and if, perchance, her eyes should fall upon these lines, let her, if she be tempted to rid herself of some "incorrigible," remember this little package of time-stained papers which she wrote and which I caught with eagerness and replied to with fervor, and all in spite of "the rules!"

(In justice, let me say that this naughty girl wrote better Latin than I did, when the correspondence began, and that this fact increased my devotion to the study of that language to such an extent that I am certain I learned

more Latin prose in writing notes to her than from the
regular exercises.)

Nor were we two sinners above all others. How is it
with *you* who read these lines? How many stones could
you throw at us if freedom from clandestine note-writing
were the measure of fitness for that sort of amusement?
I'm not saying that we did right, and yet — well, I learned
a good deal of Latin out of it all, and for some reason or
other I picked up all those bits of paper from off the
floor the other day, and put them back in the box again,
and the box on the shelf once more.

And if I should be asked now if I were sorry for
what I did so many years ago — well, what would you say
if the case were yours? What *do* you say about your own
similar escapades? Don't say that you had none such, for
if you have had interest enough in what I am writing to
read what I have written here, it is because you are " in
the same condemation."

And so let us deal with the bad children as well as
we can, remembering that out of just such a lot we came,
and see what a fine set of men and women we have made!

There is hope for humanity yet! Have we not proved it for ourselves, and is not the rule as good for the
future as for the past?

Of course I understand that things should be done
decently and in order in the school room, and that children should be controlled and *made* to do the proper
thing, if the matter comes to an issue. But don't be too
fierce to force an issue.

There are ever so many things that will take care of
themselves if you will give them time, and Mede-and
Persian laws are out of place in the school-house.

Be patient, and don't get cross yourself. Keep your
temper, and hold your flesh and blood in the background,

with your soul to the fore, and you will find the way for yourself which neither I nor any one else can ever point out for you.

For, the fact is that no one can tell you how to deal, either with bad boys or with bad boys' mothers. The evolution of the one and the involution of the other are things that you must work out for yourself. You may get a hint here and there, but it must all fall back upon *you* at last.

And, more than that, you can never hit upon any patent plan that will settle all cases of this kind for all time and in the same way. In this, as in all else, the old man's words are true, when he says: "Now, understand me well, there is no fruition of success, no matter how great, but that, out of it, something shall arise to make a still greater struggle necessary!"

That may not be a very restful sentence for a lazy soul, but it is true, and especially so in dealing with the evolution of bad boys and the involution of their mothers.

BORN "SHORT."

I wish you would stop a minute, right here, before we go any further, and think out, honestly, just exactly what it is that *you* can do, or perhaps better, what it is that you *do* do *poorer* than you do anything else in the world. Or, if that way of getting at what I am after is too galling to your self-esteem, or pride, or egotism, or what you will, all I ask is that you make a note of the thing you *can't* do, and that you know so well you can't do that you don't try to do it at all.

Now, please don't slur this over in a shiftless or lazy (not to say lying) way, but look the thing squarely in the face, for once in your life, and see what comes of it. Don't try to deceive yourself into the idea that you do, or can do, all things equally well. *You know better ;* and inasmuch as any admissions you may make here are only "to yourself" and not "out loud," be honest, and out with the bottom facts in the case, just for this once, at least.

[Pause here a full minute by the clock !]

Well, now if you are ready, we will go on.

You realize now, do you not, as a result of your reflections just made, that there are some places in *your* make-up in which you are, as it were, born "short ?" (You know "on 'change" they say a man is "long" or "short," according as he has on hand much or little of any commodity that the market deals in.)

I say you find yourself "short" on certain counts ; and not only so, but, when you come to think about it, you find that you have always been so ! That is, you are

8

not only "short" now, at one point or another, but, whatever your shortage is, *it was born with you.*

And that is what I mean when I say that you were "born short."

Just what that shortage is, in your particular case, I am not at all curious to know. That is a matter that pertains strictly to yourself, and cuts no figure in what I am about to say. All I care for is to have you realize that there is *something* (perhaps there are a good many things) that you can't do, never could do, never can learn to do with any degree of success, and that you will never even try to do if you can have your own way about it.

Perhaps you cannot sing ; may be you cannot dance, cannot paint, cannot draw, cannot spell ! cannot remember dates ! cannot remember the fundamental principles of of natural philosophy, or a hundred and one other common or curious things that some other people can do easily enough, but which you *know* you cannot do — in other words, which you were "born short" on.

Now I came across this somewhat curious fact the other day, during one of my "walks abroad," among my own mental furnishings. I was strolling along through my intellectual workshop, as it were, and taking a sort of inventory of appliances and possible output, when I became painfully aware of the real situation in my own case. I found that there were certain things that I could do, and certain other things that I could not do ; and that, for the most part, what is now has always been so, so far as primal ability is concerned.

Of course, I can do a good many things now that I could not do once. Practice and perseverance, along certain lines, have yielded fruit that is worth while. But I find that on whatever lines I was "born short," there has been no progress that is worthy the name, even though I may have striven hard to have it otherwise. I am not going to make you my father confessor, and own up, right here, just what my failings are. You who know me are probably well aware of my "shortages." I only admit that I have found several deserts and waste places in my mental field. That is all, and it is enough.

When this fact began to bear down upon me, I remembered that a wise man had said : " Do you not see that these things are the same all over the earth ? " and I began to look about me to see how it was with the rest of mankind ; I found some curious things, I assure you, some of which I am going to note, as follows :

I found a lady friend of mine who is one of the most brilliant women, in a literary way, that I ever met — a woman who fills me with wonder and amazement at the range and quality of her literary acquirements, who can repeat pages and pages from the best authors of this and other times, and whose criticisms of literature are oracles among all who know her ; and yet she cannot make change for a dollar ! She could not tell you how much eleven and a half yards of calico would cost at nine and three-fourths cents a yard ! She cannot repeat the multiplication table ! She cannot add a simple column of figures ! She never could, or did, carry arithmetic at school, and as for the higher mathematics, she has no more comprehension of their purport than has the man in the moon.

And yet this woman went to school, as a girl, and tried her best to learn numbers. She could not do it. She was "born short" on that line.

But I beg you to note that she is not a fool ! On the contrary, as I have already said, she is one of the most intelligent and cultured women I ever met, take her *in her special line of literature.*

Again, I found a primary school teacher, a good one, who has taught in the same school for years, and who has made a great success of her work, who cannot tell the time of day on a clock! This I could hardly believe when she told me about it, but on inquiry among her acquaintances, I found it to be a fact. More than this, I have since found two similar cases, one that of a gentleman, the other that of a lady. The latter has quite a family of children, and they told me that their mother always asks them what time it is, whenever she wishes to know the hour!

Again, I found a successful business man, one who has large interests in his hands and who manages them all well, who cannot go from his store to the post-office without a guide, though the places are only five blocks distant from each other, and there are only two corners to turn. His clerks tell me that he sometimes gets lost in his own store, and that they have to show him the way back to his desk! His sense of locality seems to be almost *nil*, and yet he can conduct the business of a large commercial house successfully.

I found a number of people who cannot tell one tune fr another, and many whose ears are dull when it comes to hearing a high and piercing note. I remember one man who could not hear a cricket chirping in a room where a dozen other persons, sitting near him, could hear the sound very plainly. This man was not deaf, as we ordinarily consider that infirmity. He could hear an ordinary conversation as well as any one. But he could *not* hear the high and piercing note of a chirping cricket. I also found not a few people who were color-blind, and many who were "short" in their sense of taste, and smell, and so on.

In a word, after a few weeks of pretty careful searching among persons of my acquaintance, I have made up my mind that there is not one of them who is not "short" somewhere. On the other hand, I am glad to say that every one of these same people I found to be "long" somewhere. There are not only things that they cannot do, but there are things that they can do better than they can do anything else ; things that they love to do, and are happy while they are doing them.

Of course I recognize the fact that the special cases of shortage, which I have noted at the beginning of this chapter, are very pronounced. Indeed, I do not think it too much to say that they are exceptional, very exceptional. But I confess that I have been surprised to find how many similar exceptions there are, wherever I have pursued my investigations. The quaint and curious things of this sort that I have come upon, even in a few weeks' search, would fill a very respectable volume, and it would be exceedingly interesting reading, especially if names and places were given.

And what I have done, you can do easily enough; and I think it will pay you, especially if you are a teacher, to probe about a little in this curious corner of human nature. Just begin with yourself, and when you have found out the "long" and "short" of *that* individual, you will have the key to all that can possibly come after.

Well, of course all this is only worth while, just here, on the ground that it has some bearing on the cause of education. It may be very strange, and all that, but these chapters are not a Curiosity Shop, or a place for the mere display of odd things pertaining to humanity, or anything else. And so I hasten to "call the turn" on the data which I have just noted, as follows:

I have said that I have found many grown-up people who were born short, and that neither culture nor education has availed to make good their original deficiencies.

I now beg to state that I have found many children in our *common schools* who are born short, *but whose teachers fail to recognize the fact*, or, if they are aware of it, they refuse to take it into account in the matter of the education of these same children!

That is what I want to say, and what I wish you would stop again, for a minute, and think about, right here!

It is true, isn't it? You know it is true of the children in *your* own room, don't you?

There is Mary Martin, the beautiful little brunette who sits in the back seat, and whom the whole school, male and female, raves over, but who cannot get on in her number work, though she tries ever so hard to do so. I saw this girl (and her name is legion) in a school that I visited last week. She was thirteen, and in the A grade in the grammar room. Her class was working in fractions, and she, poor thing, was doing her level best to keep within hailing distance of them.

In a bit of work that I gave to the class, I had occasion, by way of illustration, to ask them to add together $\frac{1}{2}$ and $\frac{1}{3}$. It was a simple thing, the like of which they had been doing off and on, for the last three years. The pupils were at their desks, each with pencil and paper, and each working alone.

As soon as I uttered the problem I slipped down among the children and glanced at their workings as I went. The most of them were making quick work of the poor little snip of an example, and some of them had the result before I could get to them. But when I got down to my poor little girl who was born short on this "lay" I found this: "$\frac{1}{2} + \frac{1}{3} = \frac{2}{3}$!"

Now you have seen this same, haven't you—yes a thousand times? You have had such cases in your own school many times, doubtless.   And if you have, what have you done about them?   That is what I want to know, and what I should like to have you answer to yourself, at least.

I can tell you what has been done with such cases in most of the graded schools of this county, for the last twenty years.   The fact of the shortage of this poor girl has been ignored; or, rather, perhaps, it has been held that there was no such shortage, and that the girl could be *made* to master what she had no head for.

And on this basis she has been worked, and ground, and kept after school to learn her lessons, and put back into a lower grade, all along the line, because she couldn't keep up with her class in this or that particular study,

Listen.   Great Heavens !

Or, worse than this, in many cases teachers have set such children down as fools — to use a word which seems pretty strong here, but which I have known many teachers to use in such cases.   But I want to say that these children are *not* fools; or, anyhow, they are often wiser than are the teachers who try to teach them regardless of what God intended they should learn.

For instance, in the case of the little girl I have just spoken of, her teacher told me that she excelled in grammar and in history, but that she was so dull in numbers that she desparied of ever getting her through her grade work !

Hang the grade work !   (Please excuse that expletive.   Great situations require strong language to express them.)

And, pray, what excuse can any one offer for tormenting one of God's little ones for the mere sake of having her pass in a grade?   It was the gentle Jesus who said something about millstones and certain men's necks, and a good strong rope, and the bottom of the sea, and all occupying the same space at the same time!

Brethren and sisters, will you think of these things, and reflect where you and I would now be if the above sort of justice had been meted out to us! What a multitude of millstones there would now be in deep water, surely!

Well, but you say, what are you going to do about it? We cannot let pupils go as they please. There must be some order, some method, some regularity, or we shall have nothing but chaos in our school rooms.

To which I say yes, we must have order, and method, and regularity, and all that, *just as far as it can serve our purpose, and no further.* We cannot afford to have these things *ad ex remis,* or we shall have them *in extremis!*

What shall we do then, with these "born short" cases?

Why, use our common sense, that is all. Treat these children in these respects, and in school, just as we treat them in other respects and out of school, that is all. The matter is just as easy of solution as that, when you come right down to it in a sensible way.

Just look out there on the play ground, please, where the children are having things their own way. Do you see that little cripple boy with a group of his mates about him? Poor fellow, he was born short in the matter of a spinal column, and has a pitiful hump on his back. Do you think he could ever be developed into a successful runner, and compete with his mates on such a basis? Why, even the children know better than that, and out of deference to his feelings they will not even refer to a racing game in the presence of his infirmity!

And yet, as God lives, * * * * * I am ashamed to blot this white paper on which I am writing by setting down what is sometimes done in the name of the grade, not only in the presence of, but *to* the mentally hunch-backed and sightless and deaf—the little ones who are born short!

And we can take care of these children, even in our public schools, and do for them somewhere near what ought to be done, if we only set ourselves to the task. Indeed, the very children at play put us to shame if we cannot, and do not, do this. I must not stop here (for this paper is now too long) to tell you how to do this, in detail. If you cannot find a way yourself you had better drop out of the profession, for there are still unsunk millstones and ropes, and at the bottom of the sea there is yet room for those who offend God's little ones who are born short.

Work your children faithfully and vigorously where they are "long" and strong, and help them as best you can where they are "short" and weak; and whatever you do or do not do, I beg of you not to waste your own time, and torture your victims, by trying to develop in them, severally, powers and capabilities which they can never possess.

It is not true that what *any* man has done *every* man can do. And yet the old maxim: "What man has done man can do" is generally so translated to our children, and the courses of study in our common schools are fashioned as if this old saw were one of the ten commandments.

But things are not going to be always as they now are. Will *you* see what *you* can do to set the matter right in your own school?

[Pause here and reflect for one minute, by the clock.]

HOW HE KNEW IT.

I have for a long time been possessed of a sort of latent idea, whenever I have heard certain of my fellow-men expatiating on the peculiar weaknesses and meannesses of some of their associates, that the way they happen to know as much as they do of other people's failings, is not because of their external observation of the offender they are so berating, but that it rather arises from an internal study of themselves, and their own particular "cussed-ness," which, having discovered in themselves, they very readily recognize when they see their duplicates in another. This theory of mine received a full confirmation, not long ago, from the following incident:

It happened, as I was riding on the cars, that we passed through a county seat, and a number of young people got aboard who had just been to the county superintendent's office for examination. They looked tired and anxious and for several minutes after they were seated they said nothing. Finally one of them spoke as follows:

"Well, wasn't that the blamedest lot of three-cornered conundrums, for a set of examination questions, that you ever struck?" and he slapped his seatmate on his knee with a whack that could be heard all over the car.

"Well I should smile," replied the young fellow addressed. "Wonder where he got on to 'em, anyway. Couldn't have made 'em all up himself, for there ain't a fellow this side of kingdom come that could get such a cranky lot of stuff out of his head and ever live to tell the tale. Great guns! But I'd like to get him some day where I could pop riddles into him for six hours at a stretch. If I wouldn't make him think there was retribution in this world!"

"There wasn't one in ten of the questions that I had ever seen or heard anything at all like before," remarked a bright looking young woman who sat in the seat just in front, and who turned partly toward the young man as she spoke, bringing into view a cheek that betokened health and vigor unstinted,—such a study in pink and white as one rarely sees outside of a town of five-hundred inhabitants, "There was that one about 'Sloyd!' I thought, first, it must be something about some distinguished man, for you know it was printed with a capital letter; but then it went on and asked for '*its* history and merits,' and that put me all out. I wonder if there is any such thing, anyhow?" and she aimed the question slightly toward the young man who sat nearest the window.

"Hanged if know or care," he replied. "The whole blamed thing is a humbug, from first to last, the way they're getting to run it. Sometimes I think I never will be examined again —that I will never put myself where I can be bothered and badgered till I don't know which end my head is on, and all for the sake of getting a piece or paper from a man or a woman who, ten chances to one, take 'em up one road and down another, doesn't know so *very* much more than I do, after all." And he blushed a trifle, lest, in his zeal, he had suffered his egotism to show itself a little too plainly, especially in the presence of the pink cheek, I thought.

"Oh, well, it's the law, and of course that has to be complied with," remarked a fourth member of the party, a scholarly young fellow who was standing in the aisle as he spoke. "But they are piling it on pretty thick, in some counties, I must confess; and this fellow to-day is a little the worst I ever ran against. I thought perhaps he wouldn't examine me when I went in this morning. I've been teaching for a number of years, and I hold first grade certificates from two as good counties as there are in the state. But, no! They were no good, and I had to go through the mill.

"And I never did so poorly before in my life," he added. "What with the questions, which certainly were a very "tricky" lot, and with my having forgotten a good share of the things which are generally asked at such times, but which are never used in the practical work of teaching, I made a very poor showing.

"Honestly, though," he continued, "I was sorrier for the man who was such a stickler for form, and would ask such questions, than I was for those of us who had to endure what he kept us at for the best part of the day. Such an examination is always the sign of a *little* man, and that's the kind I'm never afraid of."

"Well, but you've got to be, for he can keep you from getting a certificate, if he has a mind to, big or little," said a red-haired girl, who, up to this time, had been listening only.

"Oh, don't worry about that," returned the former speaker, "I'm here to bet that there isn't one of this crowd but what 'll get a certificate, all right and regular. You see, here's the way of it, when you come to 'analyze the causation, succession, and ultimation of the phenomena,' as the psychology professor would say.

"The very fact that a superintendent will submit such a set of questions as this man gave us to-day is proof positive that he is weak, to say the least. He has no strength in himself, and so he attempts to make us think he has by trying to paralyze us with hard and unheard of questions. So he hunts through some old books and gets a lot of 'posers' that are of no value in the world, except for just this purpose ; gets them printed, and sets us to writing on them.

"But did you notice he made the whole examination *written ?* He didn't ask a single one of us an oral question that would give us any chance to talk to him ! And that's another sign that he is a weak man, if not a coward. And if he is either, he will be afraid *not* to give a certificate to any and every person that he has been as unfair to as he has to us to-day. Such people always have a kind of low political cunning, and they make the best use of it they know how to.

"And the thing above all things that they do want is to hold their position. When such a man gets to be county superintendent, he's got a better thing than he ever had before in his life, and he'll never give it up unless he has to. What he wants to do is to make people think he is very wise and learned, and so he resorts to ' trick questions' for effect. But that is all there is of it. He never refuses to grant a certificate because a candidate can't, or don't answer his questions. He wouldn't dare to. It would expose his hand !

"So don't you worry. Your certificates'll come all right. In fact, I'll bet a dollar he'll never carefully look over a single paper that was written in his office to-day. He'll just wait a day or two, for effect, and then mail us the documents that we need in our practice."

The attendant company of listeners looked hopeful as this speaker continued, and when he closed, one of them said, addressing him : "How did you get onto all this racket ? "

The young man in the aisle paused, surveyed the group a moment, and then with his forefinger on the side of his nose, winked, and said knowingly : "*I was once county superintendent myself !*"

WHITTLING.

My grandmother was the possessor of several accomplishments that were somewhat rare among women, even in her day and generation. She was a deft weaver, and could turn out all sorts of curious patterns from her loom ; she made all the starch used in the family, and knew how to prepare metheglin ; and she could make a turkey so fat that it could not walk, but had to lie continuously on its side, in the dark, in the cellar, for two weeks before Thanksgiving !

But by far the most unique of her attainments was her ability to use a jack-knife. With this tool of tools she was an expert of experts ; and amongst the heirlooms that are still left in our family there are many silent and yet most eloquent testimonials to her ability as a cunning worker with this handiest of all implements, when in the hands of one who knows how to use it.

However, I started out not for the purpose of eulogizing my grandmother, dear old soul though she was, nor yet of writing an essay on the jack-knife and its uses, but for another purpose altogether, which I must get around to before my space in this chapter is all used up on preliminaries.

What I set out to say is, that I remember this old lady, aforesaid, once gave me a few whittling lessons that I have always been thankful for, and which I have been able to turn to most excellent use, more than once, in making m   way along the devious pathways that I have had to trudge over in my journey thus far through life. But of all the instructions she gave me in the use of the jack-knife, there was one thing she taught me that has been of inestimable value to me, as follows :

She called me to her one day and told me that they were going to make cider that afternoon, and she wanted me to whittle a plug to fit a hole in the end of the cider-barrel. She had a pine stick in her hand, to make the plug out of, and had already split it out to somewhere near the size it would have to be to fit the hole. All I had to do was to make it round and smooth. It struck me that it was an easy job, and I set to work at it with a vim —a confident boy's vim.

The stick was easy whittling, and I made the shavings curl up in great shape, the old lady standing by and look-ing on without saying a word. Presently, as I turned the stick so that I was whittling "against the grain," my knife caught too deep into the wood, and before I knew it I had split off so thick a shaving that I had made the plug too small for the hole one way ! The thing was ruined beyond repair, and there was nothing for it but to get a new piece of wood and begin all over again.

And then it was that the old lady got in her work, which has stayed with me so effectually during all the years since that far day. She said, as she took the ruined piece of wood out of my hand, " *Willie, you must learn to whittle a thin shaving !* "

And I have been trying to learn how to do *just that* ever since ; but, oh, the timber I have spoiled meanwhile, and the plugs that I have whittled at that leaked on one side because I cut too deeply there !

You whittle too, sometimes, do you not, beloved ?

Well, I see it everywhere, and especially in the school-rooms that I keep dropping into, as I go here and there, walking abroad. I saw it the other day in a school-room

away down in Tennessee. It was a young teacher that
did it — one who was as new to the business she had in
hand as I was to whittling a plug for a cider barrel, when
grandmother set me to work on that apparently easy task
— though I would not be understood as intimating that
young teachers only make mistakes of this sort. I have
seen old ones who have been at it for years, and who have
spoiled nearly every piece of timber they have put a
knife to.

It is not always a question of years and experience,
though these, of course, have great weight in the matter
of acquiring expertness in the whittling business.

This young teacher, that I was speaking of, was just
doing her first work in teaching a class to cut pasteboard
and fold it into a required form. The special work the
children had in hand was the making of a cone that should
be two inches at the base, and have a perpendicular height
of six inches.

Now it seems as though that were a very easy thing
to do ; or, at least, to teach children to do, especially as
the dimensions for marking off the pattern, and the direc-
tions for cutting and folding were all printed in a book
which the teacher had right before her all the time. It
was almost as easy as to whittle a pine plug for a cider
barrel.

And yet what thick shavings that girl whittled, and
how much timber she spoiled — or let her pupils spoil —
during the half hour I saw her at her work !

I don't know that I ought to go into details, and yet,
perhaps, it is the best way to get at what I want to say.
And now that I have written it down, I know that it is
details that I need to talk about, for it is just there this girl
broke down. She was not " up " on the *details* of what she
was trying to do. She knew what she wanted to get *done*,

but how to *do* what she wanted *done*—there was the rub.

Her pupils were well provided with apparatus and material, just as grandmother gave me a good stick to whittle and a sharp knife to whittle with. They had, each of them, a ruler, a square, a pair of compasses, a pencil, a pair of scissors, a penknife, some mucilage, a nice piece of cardboard of the required size. (These pupils were doing about the third or fourth year's work.)

Now, with that for a "lay out," it would seem as though it were an easy thing to get results that were worth while. And yet you should have seen the *results*. Perhaps you have seen the likes in your own school-room!

Let me tell the whole story. There were about forty pupils in the room, each one of whom *tried* to make a pasteboard cone two inches at the base and six inches high.

After they had worked for half an hour, I went around and inspected the work they had done. And out of the lot I found just *two* cones that were complete and of the required dimensions! That was all. The rest varied all the way from one inch to three inches at the base, and from three to nine inches in height!

And yet those children all tried (for they did *try*, all of them), to make the same thing in the same way. Their uniform purpose was to whittle a plug to fit the same sized bung hole. But oh, the leaks when the barrel was filled!

And these failures were largely the teacher's fault, and came because she did not know how to whittle a class exercise to fit the needs of her class. She had not learned the art of "whittling a thin shaving" in the class-room. When she cut against the grain of the children's ability to comprehend, she split off great chunks of lack of under-

9

standing, on their part, and what leaks resulted in their work from her blunder! Think of it, — only about five per cent. of the work would pass muster!

And yet, think not that this teacher was a sinner above all others. As said the Master about the men on whom the tower of Siloam fell, " Except ye repent ye shall all likewise perish ; " and as I look over my own work as a teacher, I can see so much glass in the house I have lived in, that I dare not throw very many stones, even at this poor girl's back window.

And still the fact remains that she was to blame. The trouble with her work was that she whittled too deep and too fast. *She did not tell the children definitely enough just what to do and just how to do it.* She told them too many things at once, and she did not take pains enough to see that they each understood just what they were to do from the word "go."

In fact, there was no word "go" about it, and that was the trouble with it all. This is what she did. She said :

" Now, children, I want you each to make a cone like this," and she held up before them a cone she had herself made, which was all well and good.

And then she went on : " Now, you want to put a dot near the top of your pasteboard, and draw a perpendicular line down the sheet, from this dot, five and one-fourth inches long.

" Then draw a horizontal line six and one-eighth inches long at the base of the perpendicular, having the perpendicular bisect this line at right angles.

" Then join the top of the perpendicular to each extremity of the horizontal line, by means of a straight line.

" Then take your compasses and set them the length of the line that joins the apex to the extremities, and draw an arc of a circle that shall reach from end to end of the base line.

"Then extend the perpendicular till it is one inch below the point of intersection of this line and the arc of the circle you have drawn.

"Then set your compasses one inch apart, and using the lower end of the perpendicular as a center, describe a circle about this point.

"Then take your scissors and cut on the diagonal lines, on the line that forms the arc, and also around the small circle, being careful not to entirely sever the small circle from the arc, to which it should remain attached."

There, that is substantially what she said, in much less time than it has taken me to write it, and it was all the directions she gave the children, other than drawing a *large* diagram of the lines on the board — a diagram which was several times as large as the one the pupils were to make.

What shavings! Rather, what chunks of mental cordwood she chopped off from the plug she was trying to whittle! What wonder the results were what they were. The marvel to me was that even two got their work right!

And yet I see quantities of such work as this in the school-rooms I go into. Of course, it doesn't all show up as plainly as this did, because the results are not as concrete as in this case — are not tangible, as they were here. But the work is just as bungling; the shavings are just as thick.

Indeed, it was not until I got out of the school-room, and began to work where I had to pay my own bills, that I realized how hard it is to teach so as to get results that will not bankrupt the teacher. But when I got into our mill, and put a boy to work upon a board that had cost me two dollars, up to the point where he took it in hand, and then had to run the risk of his ruining it by the work he had to do on it, *and I had to stand the loss if he did spoil it* — why, then the thing began to take hold of me, and I began to study the art of teaching to some purpose. And to save my costly boards, and at the same time to get the work out of the boys, that was what gave me a test of my teaching ability such as I never knew anything about before.

And yet, as a matter of fact, what are my paltry boards when compared with the timber the school teacher works with, five days in the week, for nine months in the year! It is enough to make one shiver just to think about it.

But it was a great school for me, just this working with boys and boards, and the experience taught me infinitely more about the real art of pedagogy than I ever learned from all the books on that branch of science that I have ever read.

For when, at the end of the month, our bookkeeper showed me a balance-sheet that noted a loss of dollars and dollars, and which loss came because of "waste in construction in the shop"; when I saw the cold and rigid figures which I could neither stare nor bluff out of countenance, when they looked me right in the eye and said: "You have had so much material, out of which you should have produced so much out-put, whereas you have only succeeded in getting so much out of it, and you are charged with the balance"— I say, when I saw this, and *felt* it in my *pocket-book*, why then the real condition of things took hold of me in a way that meant something.

And I wish there were some way that poor work in the school-room could be brought home to the teacher in as potent and persuading a manner as my poor shop-work was rolled back upon me. I wonder if there is any such way ? Yes, I believe there is, only it is longer in coming around, that is all. The chief difference is that the books are not promptly kept, and the balance-sheets are not taken off every thirty days, that is all.

But the books are kept somewhere, and some day they will show up, and we shall be forced to see what kind of shavings we are whittling.

How are *you* whittling, beloved ? Look at your stick, and do not forget that thick shavings mean waste and destruction and loss, and that *somebody* has to pay for all these things, *sometime.*

And happy are ye, yea, thrice blessed, if you can fashion the children that are committed to your hands so that they shall fill the places that you are set to fit them for.

Don't get blue about it, though it is enough to give one the blues, sometimes, this difference between require-ment and fulfilment ; but if you continue to whittle in the school-room, I commend to you a never-ending study of the art of whittling a thin shaving !

LIGHT, AIR, HEAT AND HEALTH.

I have been greatly impressed, as I have been in and out of some scores of different school-houses, in the past few months, with the fact that there are a great many badly constructed school buildings in this country; and because I have gleaned a good many ideas about the construction of such buildings from the many School Superintendents and Boards of Education that I have met in my " walks " here and there, and because new school buildings are constantly being erected, it has occurred to me that I might "put together a few thoughts on this subject," as we used to say in our "composition" days, that should be worth while.

What I have to say is based upon experience and not upon theory. I shall report only what I have seen and know to be reliable.

And in the first place, it seems to me that any Superintendent, or School Board that has to do with the building of a school-house ought to realize that such a building, once built, is something that will be used for a long time, and for this reason it is *very important* that it be made *just right* to start on. If it is wrong, *anywhere*, that wrong will be a constant source of annoyance, for many years. If it is right, in every point, it will be a blessing for genera-   •
tions.

And a school-house can be built that is right at every point. I make this statement deliberately, and because I have seen a number of such buildings in the past few months. That is, they seem to me to be all that is to be desired. They are well-ventilated, well-warmed, and well-lighted; the rooms are well-arranged, and the buildings present a reasonably pleasing exterior.

These things being present, what more is required?

I have seen scores of school buildings that come far short of possessing *all* these desirable things, and some that had none of them; but I have seen enough that had them all to know that it is possible to build a school house that has all of them.

And, further, I have seen enough to convince me that, if a school house is to be built it is not such a very difficult thing to build it right, if only the Superintendent or School Board get a clear idea of what *right* is.

My observation teaches me that the reason why we have so many bad school houses is because so few of those who have to do with their construction are well posted on the details of just what they should be like. These people go wrong for lack of experience.

How many of those who read what I am now writing have ever had to do with the building of a school house? Probably very few. And yet, this is a point on which school teachers, of all classes, ought to be well posted, for it is on them that school boards rely, when it comes to the practical matter of erecting a school building.

These things being so, I beg to submit a few of the results of my observation of a large number of school houses, as follows:

First, I have found that it is a good thing, when planning to build a school building, to keep in mind the fact that one cannot tell how good a school house is by the way it looks on the *outside;* and this thing is just as true when the building exists only on the architect's plans as it is after it is finished. The old maxim is true here, as elsewhere, "Handsome is that handsome does." And while an ugly exterior is to be avoided, yet no school house should ever be built for the reason, merely, that it is pretty on the outside. My candid opinion is that more bad school houses have been built from this one cause, of trying to get a *pretty looking* building, than from all others that can be named.

Hence, in settling on a plan for a school building, the adoption of one plan or another should always be determined by the inside arrangements, rather than from the outside appearance.

But this is often a hard thing to do, for *beauty* has a way of its own that often lures one away from its more practical rival, *use*. But *use* is the party to live with, through the years, all the same.

So no one ought to be deluded and waste money, and still not get what is really needed, by trying to get a *pretty* house at all hazards. Get one that looks as well as possible for the money; but have it right *inside*, at all events.

And to make a school house right on the inside, the essential points are ventilation, heat, light, and the arrangement of the rooms.

I mention these things in the order of their importance, so far as the real value of a school house, for school purposes, is concerned. I am well aware, though, that it is not the order in which these things are ordinarily counted valuable by those who have built the bulk of the school houses in this country up to date. If I should name them in such order, it would be, first, the outward appearance of the building, and, second, the arrangement of the rooms; and that would cover the most of the ground, for the great majority of the school buildings in this country today.

But as the years have gone on, and as the potency of scientific truth has begun to be realized by the people in general, gradually the public has come to understand that the first essential to a good education is good health; and to have good health with a poorly ventilated school-room is next to impossible. That is why I put ventilation as a first requisite to a school house that is built right.

And in this matter of ventilation there are only one or two things that are really essential, though people have blundered on it for years. It is really so simple that a child can understand it, so far as its practical working is concerned.

To ventilate a school-room as it should be, it is only necessary that *each room should have a separate system of exhaust and air supply*, both constructed on correct principles, as follows:

There should be, for *each room*, a *separate* exhaust-flue that can be *heated*, so as to insure an upward current of air in it; and there should also be a *separate* hot-air supply flue, *for each room*, so arranged that its supply can be taken from *any one of the four sides* of the school building.

As a rule, except in crowded cities, and often there, a school building is set in an open lot, so that the wind can strike each of its sides, as it blows north, south, east, or west; and because the blowing of the wind always affects the circulation of air in a building, this plan of taking the air supply from any of the four sides of the house, as the wind may happen to blow, must always be insisted on, to get good results.

The separate exhaust-flues should each open at the base, or floor line, of the room they are to ventilate, and the hot-air supply should be delivered into the side of the room, a few feet above the heads of the children.

With such a system, a perfect ventilation can be obtained, and with a proper heat supply (indirect steam or direct furnace heat) the house can always be kept well warmed, let the wind blow whichever way it will.

In a successful system of ventilation, then, the essen-

tials are, separate and heated exhaust flues for each room
with separate air-supply flues that can get their supply
always from the side of the house that the wind is blowing against. Such an arrangement can be made to meet
the demands of any building containing from two to
twenty rooms; and it is the only one that I have ever
seen that is perfectly satisfactory under all circumstances.

The reason why an exhaust-flue should be heated is
really very simple; and if provision is not made for heating these flues they cannot be relied upon to exhaust the
bad air from a school-room.

I have seen several very expensive school buildings,
in the last few months, that have failed to do what was
expected of them in the way of ventilation, because of
this serious error in their construction. Exhaust-flues
had been built for each room, but they were merely cold
air flues, with no provision for warming them, and for
this reason they could not do the work required of them.

Everybody knows that cold air sinks and hot air rises.
If a flue is *heated*, the air in it *must* rise; and *if* it rises,
and the flue is open into a room at the bottom, it must
exhaust the air in that room; that is, it will do so if corresponding provision is made for a supply of fresh air to
get into the room.

These two things must balance each other.

The *first* problem, in any system of ventilation, is to
get the bad air *out* of a room, and the *second* problem is
to get pure air *in* in its place. But with either one of these
two things *only*, there is no such thing as a good ventilation.

And yet there are hundreds of instances where there
is to be found only one of these essentials to perfect ventilation.

With an unheated exhaust-flue, it makes very little

difference what the air *supply* may be, since the air is more apt to flow down *into* the school-room *from* such a flue, than to be pulled *out of* the school-room *by* it. Can anything be plainer than this?

Now this is the whole philosophy of thoroughly and perfectly ventilating a school-room. It can be done in this way, every time, and it is the only way in which I have ever seen it successfully done. There is nothing mysterious about it. It is perfectly simple, and it will give perfect results.

It ought to be understood, also, that no room that depends upon the radiated heat of steam coils, or stoves, only, and is without a heated exhaust flue, and a fresh-air supply flue as well, can ever be successfully ventilated.

This is why nearly all the offices in large city buildings have no ventilation whatever. Such rooms have steam radiators, or stoves, and that is all. They are merely sweat-boxes, and nothing more.

But with a well-ventilated and well-heated school-room, the possibilities of having a good school are manyfold advanced. Without them, a good school of healthy scholars is well nigh impossible.

Given these, the next thing is the light.

There is no need of saying much about this, for it can all be told in a sentence. The light in *every school-room* should come from the left-hand side and from the rear of the pupils, as they sit in their seats. That is all there is of it.

And yet there are hundreds of very fine looking school-houses, the country over, where this very simple and easily to be obtained requisite is not present. It is a simple matter, but one that should never be overlooked in planning a school-house.

As to the size and arrangement of rooms, there is a

large space for variation on these points; but for the
average room, one that will seat about fifty pupils will be
found the most convenient. Such rooms should be arranged in the most convenient manner for getting the
pupils in and out of, and about the building, with the
least possible clashing; but this is not a very difficult
thing. I have seen less to criticise on these counts than
any other, in the buildings I have visited.

It is easy to get a good school-house, so far as all
these points are concerned; but to get the ventilation,
heat, and light right—it is a rare thing to find these what
they should be. One will find fifty handsome and well-
room-arranged school-houses in this country where he will
find *one* that has its ventilation, heat, and light as these
things ought to be.

Another item of great importance, in any school-
house, is its water-closet facilities and arrangements.
Whole volumes could be written on this often tabooed
subject. All the way from the neglected and filthy out-of-
door closets of a country school, to the ill-ventilated water-
flushed closets of a metropolitan school-house, the matter
has received but a tithe of the attention that it deserves, for
many years. But people are waking up to the matter
now, and results that amount to something are beginning
to appear.

And the most successful outcome of this problem is
the "dry closet" system, which is now being introduced
into the large majority of all the modern-constructed
school-houses. I cannot stop here to specify, but the essentials to success in any such system are, a large and
separate exhaust-flue, that shall go to the top of the
building, connecting directly with the closet at the base,
and being *heated* so as to insure a draught— this, and the
presence of sufficient heat to rapidly and perfectly evap-

orate all defecations—given these, and the problem is solved beyond question.

The rooms containing these closets should be separated from one another, so that there can be no possible communication between them, and the stairs leading to them, from the floor above, should be in different parts of the building, and as far removed from each other as possible.

Where there are two entrances to the school-house (and it is always well to have two, if possible, one for the boys and one for the girls), the stairs leading to the closets should be as near the respective entrances as possible. This makes a perfect arrangement, and one that cannot fail to give satisfaction.

There are many minor points that might be noted, but these that I have set down I believe to be the *essentials*. The height of windows from the floor—that is, having them so high that pupils cannot see out of them, is a good point to notice; but this is found in nearly all modern school-houses.

Having the upper half of the inside school-room doors of glass, is another good feature. Having the stairs that lead from the street to the school-room first floor on the *inside* of the building, is another excellent arrangement.

But this paper is already too long; yet I find it hard to shorten it and say what it seems to me needs to be said as to the essentials of a perfectly constructed school-house.

To get such a house, the testimony I have taken all leads to the fact that the architect who plans the building —its exterior appearance, arrangement of rooms, light, etc., ought also to be *compelled* to plan for its ventilation and heating, substantially according to the principles which are noted in what I have written.

In fact, whenever an architect or a school board sets to work to plan a school-house, I believe he or they can make a success of it only by *beginning* where I began this paper, at ventilation, and making all else subsidiary to that ; because it is more important than anything else, and it can be successfully provided for only when it is made the *basis of all subsequent arrangements.*

If school-houses can be built substantially "*this end to,*" the people who pay for them will get the worth of their money, and the children who attend them will be well provided for, on the physical side, whatever comes or goes; and these two things are greatly to be desired by all parties concerned.

IN INSTITUTE ASSEMBLED.

I suppose the Lord knows why it is that the good and the bad are let grow side by side in this world, so that wherever you find one of them the other is sure to be close at hand; and if He would only explain this pheno-menon, we should then know just how it happens that there are county institutes, and county institutes, all the way from those that are "away up in G," as I heard a teacher say the other day, to those that are not worth "ten cents a gross in fifty-five cent silver," as another brother (or was it a sister?) remarked in my presence not long ago, when trying to find some term near enough the zero point to express his or her estimate of the value of a certain teacher who couldn't teach.

But whatever the reason for all this may be, the fact is, that when one walks abroad among county institutes, even for a single summer, he sees such exhibitions of the good and the bad, such combinations of the just and the unjust, as to make him marvel at the possibilities in the premises at either end of the line.

A score of times in the last two months I have wished I could be a kodak, for the time being, so that I might snap-shot some of the institutes I have attended, and afterwards have the plates developed for the readers of this record; but, like the ghost in Hamlet, something has said to me that such eternal blazon must not be to the eyes of flesh and blood, and as all of the eyes I know of are constructed on that basis, I must content myself, as did the poor specter in the tragedy, by saying only "List! List! O List!"

Can anybody tell me why, in a Christian country and in times of peace, when the thermometer is 98° in the shade, a quiet and law-abiding company of noncombatant and inoffensive young men and women, mostly from the country, should be arranged in squads, and platoons, and divisions, and bastions, and breastworks, and *chevaux de frise*, or words to that effect and to the music of the wry-necked fife and boisterous drum, that make day hideous in the upstairs hall of the school house, they should be marched about and in and out of the recitation rooms like the figures in a St. Peter clock, or the automatons at Mrs. Jarley's?

I am sure it is right that all things should be done decently and in order, but when I saw such military display as I have noted above clamped on to a very clever lot of young men and women, in institute assembled, the other day, somehow I didn't like it. I saw these same young folks, when the "exercises" of the day were over, moving about, from room to room, in a quiet, orderly, and natural manner; and I couldn't help wondering why they should not have been permitted to do the same thing — *taught* to do just the same thing, if need be — rather than have been marched about like soldiers.

No, no! We don't want to make soldiers of our boys and girls. We want to make them men and women,—just plain, free, and sensible men and women,— that's all; graceful because they are natural, and obedient to the divine principle to keep out of one another's way by the use of their own wits, rather than according to orders issued from "headquarters," while the band plays!

The greatest general of recent years said, a good while ago, "The war is over!"

I wonder what has gone wrong with the first personal pronoun, singular number, nominative case, that it is no longer "good form" for a teacher to use it as pertaining to herself when talking to her class about the illustrious personage who is hearing the then-on recitation? And yet I recently heard the following from a newly-minted schoolma'm, freshly imported from an eastern teacher factory, and with the tool-marks of her makers all over her, so that there could be no mistake about the brand, as who should say, "Examine the label, which bears our signature, and without which none can be genuine!"

This young lady (and a very clever girl she was, too, after you got down through the triple plate of formality that her "training" had covered her over with) had a class of little folks that she was working, to show us "how to do it." And here is a part of what she did with that class anent the use of that least, and yet greatest of all words, the first personal pronoun aforesaid;

"Now ch'ldren," she smilingly declaimed, "look right at Miss Twiddledum (herself) for Miss Twiddledum is going to give you an exercise that will be *so* cute and funny! Now all do just as Miss Twiddledum does. That is very nice. Oh, you are so smart!

"Now see Miss Twiddledum do this! Isn't that funny?

"Now see if you can do what Miss Twiddledum did. Careful now—just as Miss Twiddledum did! Oh, no, that is not the way Miss Twiddledum did at all!

"Now look at Miss Twiddledum again! See how Miss Twiddledum does? Look sharp! Now just as Miss Twiddledum does!"

And so following, for a quarter of an hour by the stolid-faced clock which gazed at the entire performance without either smile or frown, though it was the only countenance in the room that came so happily through the trying ordeal.

10

I remember that it used to be said that President Andrew Johnson's printed messages and speeches looked like a post-and-board fence with the boards knocked off, so frequently did he use the word "I;" but even such diction seems to me preferable to the ultra " Cæsar-led-his-army" style of this latest disciple of third-personalism.

And yet double prices are paid for this sort of thing, well rubbed in, by some county institutes that I have seen!

I wonder if anyone knows just what parts of the cerebrum and cerebellum of a six-year-old child are illuminated and made to glow with an arc light brilliancy when the lucid statement is made to the little him or her that "the fishbone sound, followed by the little lamb sound, followed by grandpa's watch sound form the vocalized expression of the word cat!"

It takes *three* prices, and a "special importation of our own brand" of teachers to get such instruction as that just quoted into a county institute. And yet, though it comes high, I have found those who have had to have it, and who have had it—once! Curious world we live in, and curious folks who live in it!

But I wish you could have seen, at another institute, that motherly little woman that we all sat entranced before, for half an hour, while she taught a second reader class of boys and girls how to read.

Like Riley's "Old Fashioned Roses," "There wan't no style about her," and yet she held her class, and the fifty of us who were "observing," for thirty minutes, so that we all wondered where in the world the time had gone to.

Tell you how she did it? Ask me to tell you how the sun shines, or roses bloom, or brooks flow!

Method ? None, and all of them!

How can that be? Well, it was, and would be again, and always will be, in the hands of a teacher who knows how to teach, as she did.

That is a mystery, I grant; but it is as divine as it is mysterious.

Most divine things are mysterious—that is, they are so to a good many people, especially the matter-of-fact, cold blooded, and mathematically logical people.

This little woman was neither cold-blooded nor mathematically logical.

She loved her children (not in any gushing and demonstratively-sentimental way, but with real, honest, home-made mother love), and she had the tact and gumption to keep her children at work on a quite difficult lesson, for half an hour, by which time they had mastered it so that they could read it well, and understood what it meant.

And that seems to me to be teaching!

And for a whole roomful of country teachers to sit by and "observe" such work as that, seems to me to be a good thing. Such work makes an institute what it ought to be, and what, thank heaven, it *sometimes* is. *You* have seen the like, haven't you? *Perhaps* you can do such work. If you can, may a kind providence grant you a long life and good pay, for you richly deserve both.

————

But there are two more general characteristics of county institutes that I want to speak of, that I am sure ought to be considerably changed from their present status. And the first of these is the kind of class-room work that is done at these teachers' meetings.

In nearly every one of these gatherings that I have attended in the last two months there have been regular classes formed in all the branches of study in which

examination for a certificate is required, and most
of the time is spent in refreshing the *memories* of the
teachers on once-known-but-now-forgotten facts pertaining to these studies. The to-be teachers become pupils,
and some "professor" "coaches them for exams." as the
college boys would say.

All of which, or at least most of which, seems to me
to be far short of what *ought* to be done at a county institute. It should be to gain strength and skill as *teachers*,
and not to re-grub dead facts from their forgotten tombs
in once-familiar books, that our teachers should be forced
to come together in hot weather and work till they sweat
like harvest hands.

And the best way in the world that I know of to accomplish such an end—the only way that I believe teachers can gain strength and skill as teachers, is to have them
teach! And to this end I have seen two experiments tried
this season, which, while they were neither of them *all*
that might be desired or hoped for (what is there in this
world that is all that might be desired or hoped for?), still,
they were moves in the right direction, and were by far
the most interesting things that I have seen, in this line,
for years. The first experiment was as follows:

The institute in question held a four-weeks' session,
five days in each week—that is, it had twenty sessions.

Each day during the session the county superintendent prepared sets of tickets, twenty tickets in each set,
and had the members draw these tickets at random from a
ticket-box that was passed about the room at each daily
general session. For instance, there were twenty tickets
marked A.; twenty more marked B., and so on, in sets of
twenty, till there were enough tickets to give each member one ticket.

By the drawing of these tickets at random from the

box the institute was divided into classes of about twenty each (of course there were some odd ones, every day, for the attendance was not always in multiples of twenty, but that cut no figure in the working of the plan), and as a *new drawing* was made *each day*, of course the classes thus formed were never *twice alike!*

As soon as a drawing was made all the members who had drawn "A" tickets were sent to a room by themselves.

Those who held "B" tickets went to another room, and so on, till each class was closeted by itself.

Once by themselves, each class cast lots to determine who of the number should *teach the class* at a recitation to be held the following day, the remaining members to be pupils in the class.

Each teacher upon whom the lot fell had the privilege of selecting the subject for, and determining the scope of, the coming recitation; but each one was held strictly responsible, by the county superintendent, for the conduct of his or her particular recitation, and for the outcome of the same.

The recitations thus arranged for were each about half an hour long, and together they occupied half the time of the institute, daily, some two or more recitations being in progress at the same time; and those who were not members of the then reciting classes were observers of what was going on.

If, as the days went on, and new classes were formed, and lots were cast for teachers, the lot fell upon any member who had once been through the ordeal, a new lot was cast, so that no member had to officiate twice—any how, not until every member had served at least once.

Now, as I have said, this plan is not without its faults, and in its practical workings it ranged all the way from the sublime to the grotesquely ridiculous, from the exceedingly funny to the pathetic and almost tragic; but as a matter of fact, it did more for the young people who were part and parcel of it than anything I have seen done in an institute for many a long day.

And, above all things, it did this—it gave the county superintendent some reliable data on which to base his opinion as to the fitness of applicants *to teach.* In the case in question, the superintendent told me that he counted the work done by teachers in these test classes *one-half* in determining their grade as teachers, and I am sure it was worthy at least that much prominence.

And I wish you could have been an "observer" at some of these classes! You would have seen human nature in the school-room as one rarely gets a chance to see it. I could write for hours, descriptions of the teachers and teaching that I saw in this way.

There was the bashful girl (poor thing) who could hardly say her soul was her own, but who knew that her place for the next year, perhaps, was in the balance, and that it would come or go according as she failed or succeeded in the half hour before her. And to see her rally all her powers, and hold her timid self well to the front by the sheer force of will—men have charged into cannon-mouths with less exercise of self-control than this girl exhibited!

And there was the blasé old-timer, who has for years been able to talk off even the strong arm of the law, and get a certificate anyhow, because he could use words — he was forced to take his innings and let us see just what he could *do.* And we saw! He spent his half hour telling *how he would do it,* but he *did* nothing. And so the superintendent had the blessed privilege of, and good reason for, putting that garrulous old head in a basket, where it ought to have gone years ago.

But I must not stop to tell the whole story. To use the vernacular, "it was better than a circus." But it was sensible, and it did the work. It demonstrated whether or not those who claimed to be teachers could really teach, and that is what these institutes are for (if they are not for that, what are they for ?), and I should like to see more of the same sort. It comes nearer to being *life*, as it actually is in the school-room, than anything else I have met with.

Amongst those who were pupils for the time being there were all the shades of character that one finds in every-day school work. There were mean pupils, stupid pupils, contrary pupils, argumentative pupils, *smart* pupils, and so on, with a few really good pupils sprinkled in (which I think providence provides, so that we need not *entirely* lose heart) and the teacher in charge had to make the best of it all, just as he or she always has to do in the regular work of professional life.

Suppose you try this plan, some time. If you do, be prepared to turn pale, and to suffer from sinking of the heart at the sights you will see.

But you ought to see such sights! You ought to know what teaching, *just* what teaching the children of this country have to put up with.

And this plan will show it to you.

It will also show you *some* work that will cheer your heart, as well as, possibly, make you ashamed of yourself, as you are led to see how your very best is far exceeded by some quiet teacher whom you have never thought of as beyond the ordinary. But even such an experience is wholesome.

The plan, as a whole, is a most excellent one, and the

county superintendent who devised it not only deserves "honorable mention," but he ought to have a "gold medal" from a World's Fair.

The other plan that I spoke of is much simpler, and while it has "points," yet it is not nearly as effective as the one I have just detailed.

In this case the county superintendent would, every day, go out through the town where the institute was held and gather up a class of, say, half a dozen boys and girls, and bring them to the school-house.

He would take these children to a room *by themselves*, and there have them meet, *in his presence only*, some member of the institute, who, as a teacher organizing a school, would examine them orally, and determine what they were fit to do in the line of school work. Or, again, he would make a class of these pupils, and have his teachers, one by one, come in and teach it for a few minutes, as best they could, while he looked on.

This plan was also somewhat crude, and when I saw it in operation it had only been running a day or two, so that, as we would say in the shop, it "ran a little rough;" but it was aimed the right way, and the superintendent writes me that it was an "eye-opener" to all parties concerned. Like the other plan, its purpose is to discover whether or not would-be teachers can *teach*, and not whether they *remember* a few book-noted facts, and are able to reproduce them on paper, without referring to the original documents.

There can be no question as to whether these "New plans," or the "Old ways" are the best, and I believe it is only a matter of time when these or similar ways of determining the fitness of teachers for their work will be generally adopted. It is a fair trial, all around. If you are a good teacher, you can demonstrate the fact in

the presence of gods and men, if you have a chance to do
so; and if you are a poor teacher, it is fair that your sins
should find you out.

JONES'S DREAM.

It was the year of grace, 1893, and on the first day of
the year Dennis Dugan was plodding along on horseback
through the mud and the mist when he met, at the section
corners, Mr. Peter Jones, a neighbor, who was mounted,
like himself, and the two headed their horses into the same
lane and jogged along together.

Dugan gave Jones a " Happy New Year " as they met,
to which Jones replied in a low monotone, " The same to
you," and then became silent. The splash of the horses'
feet was the only sound heard for several rods, when
Dugan broke out:

"What's the matter, Jones? I never saw you look so
tore up in my life. You're always counted the best man
in the business for a joke; but you don't look much like it
to-day. What's the matter? Anybody dead?"

Jones looked up, gave a kind of grim and ghastly
smile, and then replied:

" No, there ain't anybody dead, but I dreamed there
was, that's all," and again he was silent.

Nothing but splashing for the next eighty rods, at the
end of which Dugan again made an attempt at conversation:

"You dreamed there was? Who'd you dream was?"

" Myself," said Jones, with a wink and a sly grin from
under his slouched hat.

"That you were?" said Dugan; and then there was silence again.

At length Jones heaved a deep sigh, straightened himself in his saddle and spoke as follows:

"Yes, I dreamed I was dead. Didn't dream much about the dyin' part, but the first I knew I was standin' afore a gate and waitin' to get in. I waited around awhile, and nobody seemed to care; so I stepped into a kind of a little office just to one side of the gate to wait.

"It was a nice kind of a room, not very big, and I was goin' around it, lookin' at things, while I was waitin'; and first I knew I saw a big book like a ledger, set up on a desk, or frame like. I kind o'wondered what it was, and as it was right out in the room where anybody could see it, I went up and looked at it, and as sure as I'm a sinner, there stood my account!

"It was headed in good style, 'Peter Jones, in account, etc.' Dr. on one side and Cr. on the other. It kind o' took me back a little to run onto it so sudden, but I'd been thinkin' about it, more or less, all the time I'd been waitin'.

"Well, nobody'd come yet, so I got to looking over the account. The first statement was, 'General Business Account,' and I don't want to brag, but I had a pretty fair showing, take it all round. I was charged up with some things, just as I deserved to be, but in the main I confess I was pretty well pleased with the way the account looked.

"Well, then came on the 'Church and Benevolent Society Account,' and that made a fair show, too. You see I've always had considerable to give, and I've liked to give pretty well, and so I've given a good deal one way and another, and it was all down, all right.

"There was one or two charges, though, on the other side, that got me a little. For instance, there was, 'neglecting meetings,' and 'giving for personal benefit,' and 'giving for the sake of public approval.' That got me a little, but I stood that pretty well.

"I went on down to the 'Widow and Orphans Account,' which was in pretty good shape, too, and I was beginnin' to feel pretty good, when I struck 'School Director's Account!' and I tell you, Dugan, my heart struck the bottom of my boots like lead. You see I'd never thought about running an account with that headin' anyhow. But there it was, and I had to face it.

"Well, as soon as I got my breath, I took a look at it. I daresn't tell you all there was there, but it just makes me sick now to think about it. Why, the Dr. columns ran on for about six pages, and here's about the way it went:

"Item—Neglecting to keep school house in repair, on account of which Geo. Newcomb's little girl caught cold and died, and several children suffered severely. [See testimony of Newcomb's little girl.]

"Item—Neglecting to stand by the teacher when some meddlesome people in the district tried to break up the school.

"Item—Neglecting to sustain the teacher when he attempted to coerce a few bad, big boys who were trying to run the school.

"Item—Hiring Mehitable Parker (you see she was my wife's cousin, and had been spending the summer visitin' us), to teach the school, she being young and inexperienced, when Hiram Samson could have been hired in her stead, he being an experienced and accomplished teacher, the change being made for the sake of saving five dollars a month.

"Item—Neglecting to visit the school and personally inspect the work of teachers and pupils.

"Item—Neglecting to confer with teacher and

patrons about the interests of the school, and so on. Here it went, page after page, all charged up.

"Item — Neglecting to insist on uniformity of text-books, and so greatly crippling the school.

"Item — Allowing family quarrels in the district to interfere with and weaken schools.

"I can't give 'em all, but they made my hair stand on end when I read 'em."

"Was there nothing on the other side of the account?" put in Dugan.

"Well, yes; clear on to the end there was just one item, and that was: 'Credit, by balance, for serving for school director for nineteen years without pay, and subject to the growls and slanders of the whole district.'"

And the old man winked slowly with both eyes, as he looked his companion in the face. He then proceeded:

"That let up on me a little, but even that couldn't make me feel just right, and I was pretty well down in the mouth about the business, when I heard the door open, and I turned around to see who had come, and it was my little girl, who came to tell me breakfast was ready, and wished me 'a happy New Year.'

"Well, I got up, eat my breakfast, but I kept thinking of my dream, and I just made up my mind that I am going to do what I can for the rest of my natural life to make a better looking record than that, when the time really does come that I have to face it. There's our school house now, with no foundation under it, half a dozen panes of glass out, a poor stove, cracks in the floor, the plastering off in three or four places, so that the wind blows right in; the out-houses without roofs, and their sides half torn off, and I don't know what else.

"I am on my way now to call a meeting of the board to fix things up, and if they aren't better'n they are now inside of a week, why my name ain't Peter Jones, that's all, and if ever I hire a teacher for any reason except because he's the man for the place, it'll be because I get fooled. Good morning."

And at the section corner they splashed away from each other at a right-angle, Jones to call the board together, and Dugan to meet me by chance, and tell me the story which I have related herewith.

FIVE OUT OF THIRTY.

I remember hearing a wise and thoughtful old actor once say: "Whenever the scenery of a play attracts the audience, and the stage carpenter becomes the star performer of the company, then the drama has to suffer."

I was in a thriving and prosperous city a few days ago, and while being shown about the town by one of the citizens, the new high school building of the place was pointed out to me. It was truly a magnificent structure and I could not help but admire it. I did admire it. I was glad to admire it. And my friend said to me:

"May be you would care to go inside and look about."

I assured him that nothing would give me greater pleasure, and so we went in together.

It was not in a western city that all this happened, as was evinced by the fact that, as soon as we were within the building, I noticed, upon the glass door, on the left of the main hall, the words "Head Master's Room." (How long a habit will hang on!)

We went into this room and there met the "Head Master." He was a fine looking, highly cultured gentleman, and he greeted us most cordially. We said the usual

common-place things for about two minutes, and then
our host remarked:

"Perhaps you would like to look over the building?"

And to this I replied: "I should be glad to do so if
we had time; but half an hour must limit my stay here,
and I should rather hear a class recite during the time
than to go over the house."

It was the look of chagrin, not to say disgust, that
passed over the "Head Master's" face as I said these
words that brought to my mind the remarks of my old
actor friend, which I have noted in the first paragraph of
this chapter. That look seemed to say that I was a goose,
or perhaps worse, to take good time to hear a recitation
(which I could listen to in any school room any day),
when I might occupy the time in going through such a
magnificent building.

In other words, this man had a very high opinion of
scenery and stage carpentry.

Of course, these are well enough, and we must have
more or less of them; but you know there are "houses
not made with hands" that are greater than any that
hands have ever made. And to see that possible architect of the divine, the teacher, actually at work with the
sacred materials that he has to deal with — to see this
anywhere, at any time, is a sight for gods and men.

And so we went to hear a recitation rather than to see
the building.

It was a class in geometry that we went to hear — just
such a class as there are thousands of, the country over,
in this great land of ours. It consisted of a goodly company of boys and girls who had got along so far in the
school course, and who were in their seats, with books in
their hands *chiefly* because it was set down in the curricu-

lum that they should do that particular thing at that particular time.

I think there were about *thirty* in the class, and of
that number, not to exceed *five* did the great bulk of the
work that was done during the forty-five minutes of the
recitation. (I over stayed my half hour.) The rest of
the class rubbed the rubber ends of their lead pencils
against their teeth, for the most part, as the minutes went
by, and, with knitted brows, tried to make out what it was
all about, anyhow.

And hard work they had of it, too, I assure you, for
not one ray of light to illumine their darkened pathway
came from the alleged luminary who sat before them
drawing $2,500 a year salary!

He "heard the recitation!"

I wonder if a man can earn $2,500 a year "hearing re-
citations?" If he can, he surely has what the great, common, ordinary, vulgar, business people of the world (the
people who pay the bills), would call a "soft snap."

And I am convinced that there are a good many
teachers, those who draw a good deal less than $2,500 a
year salary, who have "soft snaps," when judged by this
standard. One doesn't have to be very smart, or work
very hard, or be so very learned to be able to ask questions, especially if the book is right before his eyes, with
both questions and answers fairly written out.

And Oh, the teachers who teach that way! Do *you*
teach that way? If you do, ask God to forgive you, if
you can get up courage to do so, and then either better
your methods in the business, or try some other sort of
work.

Well, there those twenty-five pupils sat, and the
teacher worked away with the five who could do something with the lesson. These five were bright in mathe-

matics. One of them gave a very adroit and original demonstration of one of the theorems in the lesson; but it was chiefly Greek to the bulk of the class.

And I couldn't help thinking that there was a tremendous amount of waste going on in that school room! About sixteen per cent. of the class were getting something out of the work undertaken, and the rest "weren't in it," to use the vernacular.

Now our engineer tells me that he can utilize about thirty per cent. of the energy that is stored up in the coal by burning it under our boiler. That is a good deal better than that teacher was doing with that class, and our engineer hasn't been to college either!

And it does seem as though we ought to do as well with boys and girls in the schoolroom as one can do with the coal under a boiler, doesn't it?

So I got to thinking what was the matter with this class, and here is a part of what I thought:

In the first place, the teacher was to blame. He has a false and thoroughly bad idea of what an education consists of. He believes it to be, in the main, a good memory-knowledge of books, and, believing so, that is what he tries to make his pupils the possessors of. All his methods tend in that direction. He makes his boys and girls *memorize* the book, and *his* part of the performance is simply to see if they have done that thing reasonably well. If they have, he marks it so; if they haven't, he sees to it that they stay in the same grade another year.

Fine work that! Especially when dealing with immortal souls!

The next fault was with the pupils, more than one-half of whom ought never to have looked into a geometry. God never made them to look into a geometry. They had no faculty or sense for that sort of work, and if they hadn't, all the schools and teachers in Christendom could not give it to them !

You remember laughing at the foolish millionaire, who, when his daughter's music teacher told him that the girl had no capacity for learning music, responded: "D —n it, buy her a capacity !" We laughed heartily over that story, of course we did. That father was such a fool, and the idea of buying a musical capacity was so thoroughly ridiculous!

But how about geometry capacity? And how about the system that holds to the theory that each and every pupil must learn geometry if they are ever permitted to graduate in new clothes and have bouquets brought to them by the cart load while the audience fans itself and says "wasn't it lovely?"

But I don't want to rail, only these things make me almost wild when I see them—and I do see them, and their likes, almost every time I walk abroad and turn the knob of a school-room door.

Somehow I can't help contrasting what actually is with what I thoroughly believe might be in these cases, and when I see a class of boys and girls "worked" for an hour, and observe that, for the great bulk of them it is labor in vain, I cannot help asking myself if that is really the best thing that can possibly be done in the way of educating the rising generation. Is it? Do *you* think it is? And if it isn't, what can we do that is better?

_____

IN AN INDUSTRIAL SCHOOL.

I was once riding through a town with a friend, see-ing the sights, when all at once he remarked :

"By the way, there is something that you ought to see—our Industrial School."

And I replied, "Surely! I had rather see the inside of that establishment than all the rest of the town." And so we went to see this school.

Now I dislike to play the *role* of Momus, and it is ever so much pleasanter to say only nice things about people and places. But truth is greater than superficial politeness ; and in telling what we saw in this school I shall stick to the facts and hold them responsible for the outcome.

The building we entered is one of the best of its kind in this country. It is commodious, well equipped with all sorts of machinery, and there were nearly two hundred boys working within its walls. These boys were pupils in the high school as well, and were doing the regular course there, with this work as a sort of an extra. There was no let-up in memory work, no matter what else was done !

The superintendent of the school greeted us cordially, and detailed a member of the senior class to show us around. I do not know that the guide he gave us did by us as he was accustomed to do by others, but here is what he did for us :

He began at the bottom, and took us first to the boiler-room ; he showed us the boiler and furnace under-neath, and explained that they put the coal into the fur-nace, where it burned and made steam in the boiler ! He called our attention to the name of the firm that made the boiler, and said that it was the best firm of the kind in this country.

Then he showed us the engine, where the steam went when it left the boiler — the engine that made all the wheels in the shop " go 'round." Then he took us to the door of a large ground-floor room and let us look in, while he said : " This is the blacksmith shop." We could see boys hammering in rows in the distance.

Again, as we stood before another open door, our guide explained : " This is the carpenter shop," and we saw boys shoving planes, and there were shavings on the floor. " This is the machine shop," he said, and it was so. And in this way we " went through the building."

Finally we were brought in front of a show-case which contained some of the manufactured product of the establishment. The case was filled with beautiful things, wonderfully made, and all made by pupils of this school.

We admired these things. We were glad to do so, for they were well worthy of our admiration ; and having done this, we were escorted back to the office, and I suppose that it was counted that we had seen the establishment. Anyhow, our guide was dismissed, and the super intendent seemed to indicate by his manner that he was willing to bid us good-day.

It is a busy world we all live in, and we cannot give much time to strangers.

But the man was a gentleman, and, relying on that fact, I ventured to ask if we might be permitted to go *into* the blacksmith's shop and watch the boys at their work. The request was granted, much after the manner of the " Head Master" in the high school referred to when asked if we might hear a class recite. But it was granted, and so we went into the blacksmith's shop,

We found there about twenty boys working with the ordinary tools and apparatus of such a place. The foreman was moving about among them, and telling them what to do and how to do it; and, as far as in him lay, was seeing to it that they did as they were told. He seemed to be a very skillful man, and a most excellent teacher of the art of blacksmithing. In a word, he seemed the very man for the place.

We watched the boys for a few minutes, and then I said to the foreman: "Do you succeed in making good mechanics of all these young fellows?"

I wish you could have seen that man's face as he listened to my question. I can tell you, though, how to get a *fac simile* of it. Go to your looking-glass and stand up before it, and say to your reflected self, looking the same squarely in the eye as you speak: "Do you succeed in making good scholars out of all the boys and girls in your classes?" The glass will show you how this man looked!

And he replied, "Oh, no! *If it is in them to learn blacksmithing I can help them to become good blacksmiths. But if it is not born in them, all the shops and all the teachers in the world cannot get it into them!*"

And I thought — well, you know by this time, just what I thought. It's an old story, isn't it? But I am getting to think that it is just as true as it is old.

And then, once started, this foreman went on talking as follows: "No, I have some boys here who will never be blacksmiths. But this work is in the course, and they send the boys to me, and I have to do the very best I can with them. But it is work in vain for a good many of them. There is that boy at the last anvil in this row. He has been here longer than any other boy in the shop — has had what we call three terms' work at it; and this morning, when I gave him that piece of iron he is working on now, he asked me if it was wrought iron or cast iron!"

I looked incredulous, but the man assured me that he told the truth, and I said :

" Is he a dull boy in other things ?"

" Oh, no," replied the foreman. " He is the leader of the high school band, and I am told he is a most excellent musician. And I guess he is," he added, " though I only know about that from what others say, for I know nothing about music myself — never had any taste for it !"

And I thought —

I'm thinking yet, and I wish I could say that I had come to some definite conclusions as to just what ought to be done, in an educational way, to meet the necessities of these cases that I meet and that you meet, turn whichever way we may. Surely there must be something better than we are now doing. And, if there is, we must find it. Meantime, we will do the best we can with the old ways, and what we have ; but as sure as God lives, and as His little ones live, we will keep thinking and trying for something better.

I asked the foreman about the beautiful specimens of wrought iron work that we saw in the show-case, and which we were told came from his shop.

"Oh," he said, "that was all done by a couple of boys that were with me last year. They were perfect geniuses at that sort of thing, took to it from the start as a duck does to water !"

"Then I understand that you can not get all your boys to do such work ?" I said.

Look in the glass again !

We spent an hour longer looking about among the boys at work. I should like to spend an hour telling you what we saw, but I can not do it here. But I must say that I was greatly impressed with the idea that, for this day and age, that Industrial Training School is on the right track. It cannot make blacksmiths out of musicians, but it can make "away up" mechanics out of those who have any head for that sort of thing!

And that is what we need to-day. Our schools have been making preachers, and teachers, and lawyers, and doctors, for ages, and we are pretty well stocked up on those lines. And so I am glad to see some of the public money spent for educating our young people on new lines. For in this way — but I must not go further on the subject here and now. Why did I strike it so late in this chapter? But *you* work it out, and that will do just as well — yes, ever so much better.

PHOTOGRAPHS.

When Robert Burns wrote those oft-quoted lines:

> "O, wad some power the giftie gie us,
> To see oursels as ithers see us."

the photographic camera had not been invented. If it had been, he might have gone around to some "studio" and had his picture taken, and he would then have had what he expressed a longing for in the above lines.

Because, you see, a camera is only somebody else's eye that has the power of "fixing" the images that are made upon its retina till we can see, by looking at them, just what the pictures are like, and so, just how "others see us."

I thought of this the other day when I went into a photograph gallery to have my picture taken. I wasn't in a good mood, and the first interview I had with the camera it told me of that fact in no ambiguous way. If it had been somebody else's face that the picture-man showed me when he brought that initial plate out I should have said the mouth looked "looked cross enough to bite a tenpenny nail in two." I had no idea that I ever looked that way till the faithful camera, which could not be bribed for love or money, told me the truth. And when I found out the real facts of the case—but never mind, the story told thus far serves my purpose.

I got to thinking, as I came away from the gallery, how characteristic of the times a camera is. It shows the truth of things, no matter what they may be. Its product is not half-beautiful. Defects show just as much as perfects do.

And when you come to think about it, that is the way things ought to be shown. I know some people tell us this is not so, but I believe they are wrong. I know that some artists declare that there is no art in a photograph. Well, perhaps there is not, as they see it; but there is always one thing that seems to me fully as good and as beautiful as art, and that is *truth!*

And I wonder if that isn't the right way to look at things — just as they are, with no false light, no idealization, *so far as they are then and there concerned*, but right down to the bed-rock of the actual.

We spent several days in the art gallery, at Chicago, last summer, and as I think of those pictures, great as they are, I cannot help wondering if, after all, they are the greatest that art can produce.

I went to church last Sunday, and as I got there ten minutes early and was shown into a side pew where I could half face the audience, I had an opportunity to study the scene on my left — a small inland sea of some

five hundred faces. And I say to you now that there was
no picture in that gallery in Chicago that, to me, came
anywhere near equaling the pictures I saw in that church
during the ten minutes before the choir took their seats
and the pastor came in and the organ began to play.

It was the first Sunday for a new preacher, who had
just come to his fresh charge. And between little prayers
that were said with bowed heads, or kneeling, as the people first came in, and odds and ends of bible-and-hymn
readings that were filled in "while we waited," there was
going on, all over the church, bits of gossip about the
new preacher, and what else heaven only knows, as quaint
bonnets and curious faces leaned towards each other and
lips whispered into eager ears.

And to see those faces, and those positions, and ex-
pressions —the artist that could portray them on canvas
would be immortalized in that one act.

But the camera of my eye can portray them, and
does portray their likes, everytime it is uncapped. And
to see its portrayal is to see things as they *are* and not as
they *ought* to be; and I believe such looking is healthy
for the human soul.

And by this I do not mean that I would not idealize,
that I would take the poetry out of life; but I do mean
that, so looking, we learn to see the ideal in the actual,
and the poetic in that which, seen otherwise, would be
the prosiest of prose.

I saw a photograph of a country school the other day.
The teachers and all the pupils were spilled out on the
front steps of the school house, and the camera had
gathered them all in, just as they were. It was a picture
to look at. "The Barefoot Boy" that was done in oil
and which sold for thousands of dollars, a few years ago,
was never one-half so good as the picture of a lad that

showed up in the foreground of that country-school group.

There they were, an actual country school, with all their imperfections on their heads, and their *perfections*, too, thank heaven! There was nothing extenuated or aught set down in malice.

I both laughed and cried as I looked at the picture, as I always do when I look long at any body of faces together. All the humor and pathos of life showed on the cardboard before me. The little girl on the left was so tickled over the situation that she had to hold her hand over her mouth to keep the giggle in, and the little hunch-back boy on the top step stood behind a bigger boy before him, so that he might look as tall as any of them and still not have his crutches show!

There it all was, "down in black and white," and while color would doubtless have added to the scene, if all else that was there could have been preserved, yet, surely, no artist ever painted such a group as I stood looking at in that simple bit of light-writing. I grant that it was not ideal, but it was wonderfully real, and realities are what we have to deal with in this old world of ours, especially so far as country schools are concerned.

And, after all, are not realities enough? Anyhow, are they not enough for to-day?

I know that the *real* of *now* will be stale to-morrow; but I am coming to think that there is a better chance for *the best* to come hereafter, if we keep our eyes pretty steadily on what actually *is*.

More than that, I am coming to a place where I do not complain so much about what is, or argue so much as I once did about what ought to be. Somehow I am learning that there is a Hand behind all these things, that directs them; and if it is true that "Not a sparrow falls

to the ground without our Father," I am sure that the
rest of mankind are being pretty well looked after, even
if I do not see just how!

I think that the greatest lesson of all that the World's
Fair taught those who attended it is that things are in
pretty good shape, even as they are, the world around;
and that the chances are many to one that God has actually succeeded in making fully as good a world as any
man or set of men — society, reform club, or what not —
could have made if they could have had the fashioning of
things from the beginning!

And yet, from the way some of us have talked, in
the days gone by, it would seem as though we were quite
sure we could greatly have bettered things, if only we
could have had our own way about them.

I wonder if we could have done so?

And I cannot help wondering now how much better
we can make things in the future by our man-made and
patent processes for speeding up the car of progress, as
it were, or by hurrying the ark of the Lord along over a
highway of our own making.

I say, I can not help wondering about this. Thus, I
take some photographs of things as they were, say forty
years ago, and I compare them with some taken to-day,
and I can see a wonderful difference between the two —
between things as they were then and as they are now.
But I am also forced to see how all these changes have
come about far more in accordance with the ways of the
Powers-that-be than as I supposed they would come
about.

Oh, these photographs, that will have things as they
are, are great truth-tellers ! And the truth is always worth
looking at and studying over.

When I compare photographs of then and now, I

compare truths, and there is something solid to tie to in that. There is pleasure in it of the genuine sort, and there is profit in it too. But when you compare ideals with ideals — well, think that out.

I remember, years ago, when Mr. Horace Mann painted some ideal pictures about the public schools, and what they were going to do. I also remember some photographs of schools of many a year gone by, and I know some pictures of schools as they are in "this present now"; and, somehow, I get more insight into *just what I ought to do as a teacher* from a study of these camera pictures than I do from contemplating the perhaps more pleasingly artistic productions that Mr. Mann's hand gave coloring to, years ago.

The study of things as they are is great — yes, I believe it is the greatest.

And so I keep my eyes open for pictures of things as they are "whene'er I take my walks abroad"; and I see them, plenty of them, everywhere. They are pictures such as no painter can ever put on canvas, no artist can ever express with brush or chisel.

What studies they are, and how I turn away from them, wondering? The story that is told, and that I am permitted to read but a page of, and then must pass on, taking an everlasting interest in the denouement with me — an interest that is intensified because I *know* it can never be satisfied — these things are great to me, and growing more so, continually.

I wonder if I have space enough here to show you a few pictures that I have seen in the past few days. They are photographs that my eyes took for me, and I look at them, and question, and wonder.

It was night, and I sat beside a common "drummer" in the cars. He was an ordinary fellow. There are

thousands such. I had seen him sell goods during the
day, and had thought he was a shrewd man who cared for
business and nothing else.

But the evening wore on, and he said to me, as we
chatted : " I've been miserable all day. I was at home
yesterday, Sunday. I only get home once in two weeks.
I have a wife and two little girls at home. The youngest
is three years old. She has been more than half sick for
a week or ten days, and was very fretful, not to say cross,
all day yesterday.

"I held her a good deal of the day, but towards night
she grew so cross and stubborn that I finally gave her a
pretty good spanking. I didn't mean to do her wrong,
for she was very unreasonable and bad, and I thought she
needed what I gave her — thought it would be the best
thing for her.

"Wife didn't say anything, and when the little girl
stopped crying, she sat on my lap and went to sleep.

"Pretty soon the clock struck six, and my train left
at six thirty. I carried our baby into the bedroom and
laid her on the bed. Her cheeks were flushed, and there
was a big tear on one of them. She turned over, with a
half sigh, and threw her arms out sleepily as I put her
down.

"Wife was standing by, and just as I turned away she
put her arm around my neck and kissed me, and said: "I
wonder if you would think it hardly fair if you should
be spanked because you were cross after being sick a
week!" That's what she said, and I turned away without
a word; and, somehow, the thing has stayed with me all
day, and ridden me like a nightmare or a hideous dream.

"I don't know that I did wrong," he added, "but the
thing stays with me;" and he shook himself as though he
would be free from chains he could not break.

The train stopped, and I got out, while he went on.

But I have looked at that picture a great many times, wondering. It has a meaning that goes on and on. Many times it fills my eye, as I think it all over — the whole picture, the faults and virtues in it, all of them — and what painter ever did such work.

I was in a telephone exchange in a small town where one lone girl sufficed to do all the work required. The girl in charge was not good-looking. On the contrary, she was very plain, so plain that while I was waiting for her to call up a distant town for me, I fell to wondering if, as homely as she was, and as unsentimental in appearance, she would ever know what it was to have a lover.

Presently she got the town I wanted, and I came to her desk to talk to the party at the other end of the wire.

Now I did not mean to do what I did a second later, but it all came about before I knew it.

As I came up to her desk there was a pad of writing paper lying on it. The girl had laid it there when she took my "call" in hand; and, before I realized what I was doing I had read from that pad, "My Dearest, Darling Bob!"

To make the matter worse, as I snatched my truant eyes from the page I raised them straight into those of the girl, who that instant realized that I had seen a glimpse of her holy of holies.

And what those eyes said, and how her cheeks told stories of love revealed! Plain as she had looked to me a minute before, no painted or chiseled Venus that I have ever seen on canvas or in marble, was so wondrously beautiful, or so radiantly personified the goddess of Love, as did this common, every-day girl, as she handed me my ear-trumpet, blushed till her very neck grew scar-

let, glanced down and said "hello" to another girl fifty
or a hundred miles away.

I talked a few minutes into the instrument before me,
paid my quarter, and came away; but the picture I took
with me, and I wonder if I have let the light strike
through its negative upon this page so that you can get
a glimpse of it.

However, its likes are everywhere for those who have
eyes to see them.

One more, and I am done.

It was night again — midnight. I was waiting for a
train, and a wise and staid old schoolmaster of sixty-five
winters and summers, a man who had seen some forty
years of service in the school-room, was waiting with me.
The waiting-room was still. We were the only occupants.
The lights were low and we talked in an undertone, our
voices echoing in the bare apartment. Finally the old
man said (he is a model of all the virtues, especially the
colder ones):

"I visited my old home in Vermont this summer —
went back to where I was a boy more than fifty years
ago."

He drew his well-brushed silk hat down over his eyes
a trifle, and slipped down into his seat as he spoke.

"Things have changed a great deal from what they
used to be," he went on. "They have a railroad now
that goes right through the old farm where my folks used
to live. We went whizzing by the old place the other
day, and just before we got into the small village, where
we used to go to trade, we passed the little old red school
house, where I got all the schooling I ever had till I was
of age. It is a small brick house, and stands just at the
foot of a hill that runs up an easy grade, just behind it,

perhaps fifty or seventy-five feet high. It is a sort of sandy hill with rocks sticking out here and there. "

The hat came lower over his eyes which were now closed as he went on:

" Right on top of this hill, back of the school house, there is quite a clump of large pine trees, such as grow to perfection in that barren soil, and in just such places as this hill-top. They were there forty years ago, those trees, and they are there to-day — don't seem to have changed so very much in all that time."

The hat fell forward more and more, and a little over one eye. It seemed to be "cocked" just a trifle, I thought, as I remembered the scene.

" I noticed those old trees as we ran by in the cars the other day, and it all came back to me as though it were but yesterday. I remembered that there used to be some rude benches under them, and that we children used to go up there noons and eat our dinners; and then I remembered" (the hat fell over one eye and took upon itself quite a jaunty air) " How — let me see, I must have been about seventeen; no, I guess I was eighteen — how I went out walking one clear, moonlight night in June with a little girl I was going with then! She was a sweet little thing, plump," (the hat tipped another notch) "rosy-cheeked, black hair and eyes. I can see her now just as she was then.

" We strolled down to the old school house and up this hill, and sat down on one of those benches. I don't know how long we sat there. Time isn't paid much attention to on such occasions. We didn't say much, but finally, I remember, *she gave me a kiss!*"

You should have seen that hat!

" I remember," he continued, " how timid she was

about it, as though she wanted to give it but was almost afraid to."

There was a rumbling outside as the train rolled in, and ten minutes later we were both in our berths, rushing headlong into our dreams at the rate of fifty miles an hour.

But that picture!

Or, rather, the two pictures — the then and the now. The one, the decorous old schoolmaster, the properest of all proper men. A grandfather whose grandchildren have in their veins no trace of the blood of "the sweet little thing" who sat with him on the bench in the moonlight nearly fifty years ago; the other of the boy and the girl who sat there. Photographs both; and what artist, other than a camera that sees things as they are, and has power and principle enough to reveal all that it sees, just as it is, could have sufficed for those two scenes?

Yes, I like photographs. I like life as it really is. I like the truth. Who is it that says: "I do not want the constellations any nearer. I believe they are well where they are, and will be well when they have moved on," or words to that effect? The ideal is good to dream of, but the real is the thing to live with.

When you look at your schools, beloved, let your eyes be the cameras that shall see what is to be seen. Let them take pictures for you — pictures of things as they are, in deed and in truth, and then, when you are alone, look the prints over, and see what there is in them.

You may not be able to have an "Angelus" on your wall, but you can have a thousand better things in your heart's secret chamber — pictures that shall stay with you here, wherever you are, and perchance adorn your "'mansions on high" on the other side.

HALF-TONES BY THE MILLION.

What a curious fad that is which expresses itself in the preference some people have, or profess to have, for things that are "hand-made." There is my lady at the ball who spreads and swells herself with pride over a bit of lace which she boasts was "made by hand" on a pin-cushion rather than on a loom in a factory. I know a gentleman, too, who wears a watch-chain whose links he tells me are "hand-hammered." It is so heavy, to be sure, that it breaks all the button-holes out of his vests, but it is "hand-made," and that atones for all its clum-siness.

These are two instances that might be made two hundred or two thousand, but they are enough for my purpose, since they illustrate what I have in mind.

I have been thinking about this peculiar phase of human nature for a day or two, and trying to account for it. And here is what has come to me. I think it is a rather pronounced out-cropping of ultra-individualism, which borders pretty closely on the confines of absolute selfish-ness. It is a sort of mania for owning something that no one else possesses or can possess.

Perhaps it arises from the fact that no two of us are alike, and so we, as it were, naturally prefer that our be-longings should smack of ourselves. But, if even this is the source of the characteristic, and so may, in a measure, be good, yet I am certain that it is a quality that can very easily be carried too far, and that very soon reaches the region of selfishness, pure and simple.

12

And selfishness, pure and simple, is the very thing that this age seems set to overcome. The vital breath of this era is democracy; and this, in its essential principle, is the very antipode of selfishness. It is everything for everybody—not everything alike, forsooth, but enough of every good thing to go around. It is not what I can have alone by myself, but what everybody can share with me. This is the kernel of Christianity, the soul of the brotherhood of mankind.

I thought about this the other day when I went into a modern engraver's establishment and saw the artists there at work upon some "half-tone" plates for reproducing, to the very slightest detail, several great works of art that have for years been the sole possessions of certain individuals or societies. It is a wonderful process. There is very little "hand-work" about it. The sunlight is the artist and it does such work as no human hand can ever rival.

It is the photograph business again, only this time for the masses, the millions. It makes the world familiar with the faces of those whom we are all anxious to see and to know about, and it is little short of a miracle how accurately and perfectly it does its work.

Well, I stood and watched the process whereby a rare charcoal sketch, by a celebrated artist, a picture that has long been the sole property of a friend of mine, was virtually "cut in brass"—transferred to a plate from which a million duplicates can be made by machinery, and every one of them a better copy than ever could have been made by hand.

And I was glad of this beyond all telling, for the picture is one that to look upon "doeth good like a medicine," and I am rejoiced that the multitudes can have the pleasure that must come even from viewing its "counterfeit presentment."

I asked the 'artist if he could make "half-tones" of any and all pictures, old, new, and what not. "O, yes," he said, "if only the originals are well defined. The sunlight is no respecter of times and places and people; all it asks for is a fair opportunity to do its work. Meet its conditions and success is assured."

My reason for asking this question was, that I have in my possession a number of pictures, some old and some new, that I should like to have "half-toned," that I might share them with—well, with everybody who may care to look at them.

And so, partly by way of experiment, I had an old pen-and-ink sketch of forty years ago put through the "half-tone" process, and here is the result. Possibly some of your school children may care to look at it with you. If so, I shall be doubly paid for having had it reproduced. So here it is, as follows:

THANKSGIVING.

Thanksgiving now is not just what it used to be. It used to have a characteristic quality, which was that on that day everybody went to grandpa's. Three generations always met on that day. And there was always a house full, for plenty of children was the rule and not the exception when Thanksgiving was young.

It always snowed just a day or two before, and the first grip of genuine winter came just in time to freeze up the piles of mince pies that were baked the week before Thanksgiving. The first sleigh ride of the season always came when we all went to grandpa's, on that great day of the year.

Grandpa lived up in the hills, a good day's drive, and

we always used to go up the day before, on Wednesday. We had to get an early start, and the last stars had not been put out for the day when we were off. How the bells jingled and the horses' feet crunched the shining road, and the runners squeaked over the frosty way!

We had to get out and walk over the covered bridge, because they hadn't put the snow on for the winter yet. But how we were tucked up when we got in again, and how good the warm stone felt at our feet!

Then, away we went, up hill and down hill. Mary's ears grew cold, and mother's muff—a great, big, fluffy muff, but ever so warm—held to them was the only thing that would keep them from freezing. But away, and away, we went! The sun came up, and we sang, "Away, away, away we go." Mother sang, father sang, and we all chimed in.

That was just where the road turned and went down hill into the woods and across the brook that never froze over, it ran so fast. Goodness! how the echoes rang! I can hear them yet, though half the voices that sang on that morning are now still and have been for long years.

After that the hills grew steeper and we went slower. Then we got hungry and had lunch—seed cakes!

And so the way wore on till about two o'clock, when we got to grandpa's.

The old man stood, bare-headed, at the gate, the wind tossing his scanty hair. As we drove into the yard he jumped on the side of the sleigh, like a boy, and came piling down on top of us with a romp, as we moved up to the front door. Then he took us out and kissed us. How the whiskers pricked! for it was Wednesday afternoon and he hadn't shaved since Sunday.

Into the house to meet grandma, uncles, aunts, and cousins, a troop of them, and for every one a place and

love without stint ! Up to the old fire-place, with its generous blaze of hemlock and hickory—was there ever such
cracking and snapping as used to welcome us at the old
hearthstone !

We had an early supper and then went out to see
grandpa milk. He used to put on an apron to milk in,
and we thought that was because he was a minister, and
so something like a woman. He milked, making two
streams beat time in the pail as if they were one, and not
alternately, as father did, and that was a wonder. Then
into the house again to wait till it got real dark, when we
were to see the turkey killed.

Thanksgiving and turkey ! Indissolubly one !

So, when it was real dark, we went with grandpa to
the barn. Out through the woodshed, and the shop, and
the carriage house, and the corn house, clear to the barn
without going out doors ! What a line of boys and girls !
Fifteen of us, and the oldest not twelve—unless you count
grandpa ! He led the van, with the lantern—the tin lantern punched full of holes that the light could shine out
of, but the wind couldn't blow into.

All in, and such a row of little heads, covered with
aprons and towels and what not ! No wonder the old
mare poked her nose over the manger and snorted.

But hush ! The old gobbler sees us, too, and pokes
his head out, and turns it up to one side. Walter takes
the lantern, and grandpa steals up in advance. A breath-
less silence, broken by a flop and a tremendous flutter,
and the old fellow is on the floor. Then we all rush up to
see the poor creature blink in the lantern light, and gaze
on us in such a helpless way. But *we* can't help it !
Think what he will be to-morrow !

And away we go, back to the wood-house, where the

old fellow goes bravely to the block for the cause; then into the house to see him picked; and then to bed.

Yes, to bed! Three in a bed all around! We all undressed down stairs, hiding, modestly, each behind his mother's chair, as she sat with her back half turned to the fireplace.

Nightgowns all on and feet all bare, we stood before the fire to see who was tallest, Ophelia at the head and Lily at the foot — the stalk broke that winter and Lily died.

Then, as we stood there, grandpa came up behind, and spread his hands out over us, and gathered us all into his arms and about his knees. The tears trembled in his eyes, and with stifled voice he said: "I thank thee, Oh Father, for all these little ones; oh, bless them, every one. Spare their precious lives, if it be Thy will, and help them to be good boys and girls, and to grow up to be good men and women. Amen."

That was the prayer, never to be forgotten. How still we all stood for a minute after the amen was said, till grandpa stooped over and kissed Flora. That broke the spell, and we all began to kiss all around.

And such kissing! So many kinds! Uncle George had just come from the far west — St. Louis! — and had a great long moustache. How it tickled! And aunt Minnie's soft lips, and aunt Flora's fat lips, and grandma's wrinkled cheek, and, last of all, grandpa. Then, off for upstairs!

Ah, but the stairs were cold! -- had oilcloth on 'em! Then into the great, high beds — feather beds and woolen blankets; and grandma had warmed them with the warming-pan! (Can anyone tell why that luxury has been forgotten?)

All snug in bed. Good-nights repeated again and

again, and sent in packages to the folks downstairs, the door is shut. It is dark; Walter tells a ghost story, Wallace tells another; then, one by one, we say our prayers. Almon says "trespasses" instead of "debts;" but we all agree on "Now I lay me." Emma begins another story, but it's too long, and we fall asleep, one by one, till, finally, she yields herself, and her eyes close with her mouth full of words. And we dream.   *   *   *

Morning — Thanksgiving morning! Who shall write the record of the day?

Down stairs to dress by the fire! Breakfast! Such cakes! And we all have coffee! Then prayers. We all have bibles. All who can read, read, each in turn; and the little ones who cannot read, say over a verse, word by word, as it is read to them. And then the prayer! Surely such prayers as grandpa prayed are answered. He called us each one by name, and asked God to bless us and help us to be good. None that heard that prayer will ever forget.

Prayers over, there is a break for the kitchen, to see the turkey stuffed and put into the brick oven; to crack nuts, stone raisins, bring in wood, and help (?) do a hundred things. And that brick oven! What fragrance came from its spacious recesses when its mouth was opened and disclosed, side by side, the turkey, two Indian puddings, and an immense chicken pie! That was Thanksgiving!

Then, when all these were in the oven, we all made ready and went to church. Grandpa preached. First he read a psalm that had the word "thanksgiving" in it. Then the choir sang an anthem in which tenor, treble, alto, and bass, scampered after each other with the words, "with thanksgiv-," "with thanksgiv-," "with thanksgiv-," in a regular race; till, finally, when they had worn each other out in the chase, they all came together on "ing," and then sang "amen," and retired behind the little green curtain that was stretched before them.

At last it was over and we were back again for dinner. This was the climax. We children "waited," but that was nothing. We had the sitting-room all to ourselves, and we had no end of fun. We played "Robin." Do you know "Robin?" It is an old game. We got a short pine stick, half as big as your finger, and stuck one end into the fire till it blazed. Then one of us took it and said: "Robin's alive and live like to be; if he dies in my hands, you may saddle-back me."

As soon as he said this he passed the blazing stick to the next, who repeated the same words, and passed it on, and so on round. When the flame went out "Robin" was "dead," and the one in whose hands he died had to be "saddle-backed."

Saddle-backing meant that he should be laid on his face on the floor, and all the chairs, and tables, and stools, and whatsoever in the room, should be piled on top of him. No wonder it seemed a short time that the older folks were at dinner.

And then came our turn. The table was re-set, and one Indian pudding was left untouched for us. How we ate! The turkey and chicken-pie were so good that Henry ate his fill of them; and when the pudding came, and the tart pie — with little scallops and rings on top — and mince pie, and pumpkin pie, and plum cake and nuts — he could eat none of them, and cried because his stomach was so small.

Then grandpa came behind us, with his hands full of raisins, and we put our heads back and opened our mouths, like birds, and one by one he dropped the fat plums between our lips.

And so the dinner ended. Apples and cider and nuts came later in the day, as we sat in a large circle around the old fireplace. Then, evening and games —" 'Pon honor "— and such a pile of hands on grandpa's knee! and such awful questions as were asked the unlucky ones! "Whom do you love best?" and one said Lucy Trow, when down in his little heart there was rebellion, because he knew he ought to have said Eliza Winslow, for hers was the image he cherished there! Ah, pure and true little heart, that rebelled at even a seeming denial of its love!

And then a romp with grandpa! Down on his hands and knees (he was seventy-four) and he was our horse. In behind the lounge, he was a bear. How he watched from his den, and sprang out and caught us, poor little lambs, and ate us up and wanted more! Then blind-man's-buff, and so on, game after game, till our little eyes were heavy; then bed and a child's sleep.

Morning again. Breakfast and prayers; then good-bye, and off for home. That was the Thanksgiving of the olden time.

HONORIFICABILITUDINITY.

I have been trying my hand a little at the census business, or perhaps consensus would come nearer expressing what I have been attempting to find out.

For a long time I have been greatly interested in the matter of teaching reading in our public schools, and because " the proof of the pudding is the eating, " and that the further fact remains that a "workman is known by his chips, " I have been tasting the reading puddings, so to speak, that our schools are now making and baking; and examining the chips that fly off as our teachers " hew to the line " in the reading classes, let what will come of it.

And here are some of the things that I have found: To begin at the beginning (and let me say, right here, that my report will, for the most part, like all other census reports, merely state things as I found them, leaving other folks to form conclusions therefrom), I started out with the purpose of asking *primary* teachers just two questions, the first of these being, What method of teaching reading do you use ? and the second, Will you tell me *your own private opinion* about the real merits of such method, based on your own experience, and unbiased by anyone else's opinion or say-so ?

With these two questions formulated I set out on my census pilgrimage.

I had almost no trouble at all in getting prompt and unequivocal answers to the first of my questions. Whenever I propounded the same, the reply would come back at me as a ball comes back from the bat, and always straight at me. There were no " fouls " made, no "strikes " called. It was a straight pitch and a square bat, every time.

And in almost every case, north, south, east or west, in city, town, or country, I got one of two replies. Either my respondent would say, "I use the word-method of teaching," or "I use the sentence-method." There were some slight variations in these replies, some teachers working in a personal adjective in their answers, as "I use Brown's word method;" or "I use Jones's sentence method;" but this seemed to be a small matter, so far as the general trend of methods was concerned.

In one or two cases I got a reply, albeit from rather old-fashioned folks, "I use the alphabet method;" but the great bulk, at least ninety-five per cent. of the teachers I put the question to, answered either "word-method" or "sentence-method."

And so my census, on this first question, seems to have determined this fact (for I took schools at random in some twelve different states) that the great bulk of our primary teaching of reading is now done by the "word method," or the "sentence-method." I consider that point fairly established. I make no comments; I only record the fact.

But when I propounded my second question, then came the rub. To return to my base ball figure of speech, it seemed almost impossible for me, at first, to get anybody to "bat to my pitching" at all. Some would strike towards what I said, but would take great pains not to hit the real issue by so much as a "tick." Others would "swipe" my interrogation clear out of bounds on a "foul," and baffle all my efforts to get them to really "play ball."

But I finally got what I wanted. I am not a Mason, but by working the "never'll tell," secret service system on my reluctant non-respondents, I finally began to get results. These results I am glad I am now able to make public without betraying those who reposed their confidence in me, since all the pledge I gave them (and, indeed, all they asked me to give them), was that, in anything I might hereafter say, I would not reveal the *identity* of my informant.

Curious fact, that; that we all hesitate to give an honest *personal* opinion unless we can run to cover under an *in cog. !*

Well, when I had finally found the way to get any replies at all to my second question, the answers came with a uniformity that was somewhat remarkable, to say the least; especially in view of the reluctance to respond, noted above.

With a *very* few exceptions, which I can readily account for, the replies all agreed on the following points, namely, that these two systems of teaching reading tend to make excellent *vocal* readers of reading matter, the words or sentences of which have been *told to the children to start on;* but the pupils thus taught do not read *new* matter well, and they do not *spell* well.

How is it in your case, beloved ?

The census I have detailed is neither an imagined or a fanciful statement. It is on the bed-rock of the actual; and, being so, it seems to me to be worthy of some special consideration.

And what I am anxious for is that it should have the special consideration of the *rank and file* of primary teachers, because it is they who know more about it than anyone else. This may not seem so at first, but think about it awhile and the light will appear.

To help out on that line a little, the line of theorist versus the actual doer of the thing theorized about (call them superintendent and teachers, if you would like to), let me quote from a letter that lies before me. The man who writes it has been a superintendent of city schools for many a long year, and is among the best of the lot, and he writes me thus:

"I want to tell you of another new continent that I have discovered, pre-empted, and explored second-handed.

"I have been reading for the past four or five years of the wonderful discoveries by a few of the leading educational thinkers who have been studying their children, their grandchildren, etc., and I have been charmed, elated, almost transported at the wonderful facility with which these little prodigies have absorbed and reflected knowledge.

"More's the pity, bloated with this information, I have gone systematically to work to make the life of my primary teachers an absolute desert of misery and dread, by requiring them to do as much work as was accomplished by these little prodigies of perfection.

"It is quite likely that I should have gone on at this nerve-straining rate to the end of my superintending career had not the Good Father sent one of those sunbeams to gladden my life, in the shape of a flesh-and-blood boy. Like his father, he refused to be a prodigy, and I have discovered, in my efforts to find what he knows and what he can do, that he is many degrees removed from the perfection outlined by Perez and others of his kind.

"I think I have learned more about how much it takes to teach some children a few things than I could have learned from a stack of books high enough to enable me to see into the Promised Land.

"I think, also, I shall hereafter be more humane to my primary teachers, in fact, to all my corps of assistants, than ever before."

There, I think, that is a pretty fair setting forth of "Theory *vs.* Practice."

And there needs to be just such a rounding up of these two, every now and then, if they keep in line as they ought to. This theorizing business, especially when it takes analogical reasoning along as a partner, is apt to very soon become a gay deceiver, and to leave its votaries in all sorts of predicaments, just when they are feeling cocksure the next step will land them in the millenium.

And so, to come back to that cold and heartless census report (for such the like always are; but it is they that put the ultimate test to all theories), these primary teachers, who have honestly given me their own private opinions about the *real merits* of the present system of teaching children *to read*, have brought out some facts that must give all theorists about the matter something to think of.

And just here will you kindly oblige me by pro- nouncing, instantly and at first sight, by either the word- or sentence-method, whichever you prefer, and without having anyone tell you what the word is, so that you can say it over after them, the following:

Honorificabilitudinity !

And if you fail to fetch it on sight, the first time, I wish you would reflect just a little as to how you will finally "down it." For you will finally down it. And when you have done so, just stand off a little ways, so that you can put the act into perspective, and see how it was that you did it. And then you will please ask yourself if the methods of teaching primary reading that you are using in your school are enabling your pupils to "down" *new words* when they come to them, without someone's telling them what they are ? Just think it over, that's all.

And that is what I got out of *that* part of my census work.

As I pursued my investigations in the higher grades I took a little different course. I kept tab on the number of pupils who, as they regularly read in their classes, read right along, easily, and in such a way that their pronuncia- tion of the words indicated that they understood what it was all about that they were reading from their books. And on this count I will, if you please, report rather my own impression than state, numerically, the results of my work.

After watching the point carefully for months, I am convinced that the average reading book, above the third reader, is much too hard for the average pupil. The themes are, many of them, too lofty (I guess that is the word), and especially the poetry is beyond the range of vision of the average pupil.

And I must insist that it is the average pupil that we must keep in mind in all these things. Who are our schools for ? Sometimes I am led to think that they are only for the bright pupils, whom we want to fit for college!

I wonder if it is so ?

And in the higher books this difficulty that I have noted seems to grow worse. Indeed, as I think about it, I fear the evil (if such it be) is one of pretty long standing. I have a dim and misty recollection about " Webster's reply to Walpole, " or " Pitt's reply to Hayne, " or something of that sort, that I was set to wading through at about eleven years of age. The exercise evidently made a lasting impression upon me !

But here is the chief point that has impressed me about all that I have seen or sought to see regarding the teaching of reading. We spend the great bulk of the time that we devote to such teaching in the public schools upon vocal work — to teach the pupil to read aloud; when the fact is that *not one per cent. of all we read after we get out of school will be oral reading!*

But the art of reading well silently, of getting the thought out of the words upon the page as a bee gathers the honey out of a flower — how much time and attention do we devote to that? How well do we teach our children to read books to themselves? What plans are we working to that end? Is it worth while to have any special plans to accomplish such a result?   If the great bulk of the reading we are to do in life must be *silent* reading, is it wise to keep that fact in view when teaching reading in the public schools?

These are things to think about.   Not for superintendents alone, but for the rank and file — for *you* in especial.

But it is a question, how to get results out of the reading class that are satisfactory, all along the line. Children are so different about learning to read, aren't they?

Why, we had a little girl five years old, at our house this last summer, who took Carlyle's "Sartor Resartus" off my library shelf and opened it at random, and read right down the page as "Tammas" himself might have done.   The little button of a thing; I don't believe she would have weighed forty pounds, all told, and yet she read like an antiquary.

She has never been to school.   She isn't old enough to go to school.   No one ever taught her to read.

Next year she will be old enough to go to school.   I wonder if she will be sent to the chart class, and have to say " I have a cat," while she whisks the pointer across the blackboard where the *chalk* says "I have a cat!"

I don't want to say a mean thing, or be sarcastic, but some of the things that I see as I go about make me want to say something.   And the question is, what shall be done with this little girl when she goes to the reading class next year?

I grant that her case is exceptional, wonderfully exceptional, and that the general trend cannot be set aside for the entirely unique.   But yet?

On the other hand, there is my neighbor's boy, who, at eleven years of age bungles along at a snail's pace in the second reader.   He, too, is exceptional.   But both these children will be at school next year, possibly in the same school (they or their similars), and what shall we do for them? That is the question.

Well, if the system won't take too strict an account of them they will be provided for. You could care for them both, and keep them both growing, couldn't you, if you could have your way about it? I think so.

And I wonder if that isn't the thing to do. I believe, too, that you can be permitted to do it if you will be as frank and honest with your superintendents as you have been with me in answering my questions. If you will tell them what you honestly think, as you have told me what you honestly think, it will help matters amazingly. It will do them good, it will do you good. Don't be too " brash," or too rash about it, but honestly, quietly, conscientiously say your say, and it will have its weight toward making your school better, beyond question. Try it. Not too hard; but just a little, to see how it will work.

And now you will say that I haven't told you how to teach reading. And I haven't. Nobody can tell you how. All anyone can do for you is to give you an ink ling, and then you must work it out yourself. That's the way God has made things in this world, and it is that way or none.

" No one can grow for you — not one. No one can acquire for you — not one."

·   All I can ask, or hope for, is that you think over my census, look over your own work, and see if there is anything for *you* in what I have said. And if there is I shall be happy.

------ ---

SQUEAKS AND GREASE.

I think I have said it before, but I cannot help saying it again, that, *when a machine squeaks, the place to put the grease is right where the squeak is, and not all over the whole mill promiscuously.*

The particular reason why I repeat this oleaginous bit of philosophy, just here, is that I have seen so much good oil wasted, in the last few weeks — so many school-rooms and school children slobbered all over with superfluous grease, as it were, that I have become almost heart-sick at the sight.

I wonder what a recitation is for, anyhow? It would sometimes seem as though its chief aim was to serve the double purpose of killing time and muddling pupils up — "knocking them out," I am almost tempted to say.

I don't want to seem harsh or out of patience, or to say mean things; but as I drop into schools here and there, going about the country as I am now doing, I see things of this sort, such multitudes of them — I see such oceans of wasted school-grease, so to speak, stuff that not only does no good, but smears and litters up what would otherwise be clean floors and reasonably clean children, that it is hard to keep one's mind in a composed state.

And all this wastage costs so much !

My grandmother taught me that it was wicked to waste, and I know that her precept is true. It *is* wicked to waste; and like all other wickedness it will bring its reward in time — it will result in bankruptcy some day, if something is not done to put a stop to the waste.

But to the point:

It was a second-reader class that I saw. The pupils were required to write ten "commanding sentences" on their slates. There were some ten or twelve pupils in the class. They came to the front, slates in hand, the sentences all written, and the exercises proceeded as follows:

Pupil (reading from slate) -"Shut the stove door. Commanding sentence. Begin with a capital and end with a period!"

Teacher—"Can you not make a better sentence than that?"

P.—"I don't know."

T.—"Would it not be more polite to say, close the stove door?"

P.—(Going on without further remark)--"Close the stove door. Commanding sentence. Begin with a capital and end with a period." "Shut the outside door. Commanding sentence—Begin · with—a—capital—and—end—with--a period." Go to school. Commanding—sentence—Begin--with—a--capital--and—end—with--a—period " "Go to town—C—s—B—w—a--c--a--e—w—p." Get the book- C s—B—w—a—c—a—e—w—a—p—." "Get the hat—C—s—etc." "See the man. C—s—etc.' "See the hen. C—s—etc." See the pig. Commandingsentence Beginwithacapitalandendwithaperiod!"

T.—"That will do. Mary you may go on."

Mary—'Get the book. Commanding sentence. Begin with a capital and end with a period," etc.—etc.—etc.—etc.—etc.—etc.- etc. —etc.—etc.—etc. etc. -etc.—etc.!

A good many of them, are there not?

That is just what I thought before the fifteen minutes ended that brought this jargon to a close.

In heaven's name, what excuse can possibly be offered for the like of this? And I have given it just as it took place, only I haven't set it all down yet.

The class, having gone through this "exercise," was dismissed, each pupil handing his slate to the teacher *en route*.

The teacher took the slates and hastily ran over each one, and with a pencil checked some of the errors on them —that is, if the child had written a "declarative sentence" instead of a "commanding sentence," she put a cross after the offending member.

That was all!

Then she marked the slates, transferred the marks to her record book, and returned the slates to the pupils without a word!

Fact!

And yet this woman is a member of church and society in good and regular standing, virtuous, and ostensibly anxious to earn her money. I really think she was trying hard to teach school.

But was she teaching school? That is the question. Is she a *teacher* at all? Look over the record of her work and see if you can find any sign of *teaching* about it, anywhere. (And when you get through looking over her record, just cast an eye over your own, please).

I went down and looked at the slates which had just been returned. The first one was the property of a little fellow named Eddie something. His name was at the top of the slate, spelled Eaddie! Further down he had written the sentence, "Go to bed," which showed thus: "Go to bead." A little further down the list the word "fed" occurred, which was written "fead."

Now it did seem to me that this teacher ought to have noticed the *squeak* there was in this boy's spelling machine, and then and there applied a bit of grease, right on that particular "ea," that will make him all the trouble of a very disagreeably "hot box" one of these days, if it is not lubricated before long.

He had said "Commanding sentence. Begin with a capital and end with a period" *ten* times, in the class (and dear only knows how many times he had said it before, and may have to say it again before he can graduate in new clothes), and yet the "ea" for "e," which is evidently a chronically hard place in his spelling economy, goes squeaking along, unnoticed, day after day.

And the other slates were only partially better. There were squeaky places on every one of them, but not a drop of the oil of teaching-where-teaching-was-needed did I see poured on a single squeak. It was all dumped out in one general pool, over the whole class, for fifteen minutes, as pupil after pupil rattled out, "Commanding-sentence-Beginning-with-a-capital-and-ending-with-a-period."

I wonder how Gabriel will enter up the record of that alleged recitation? Anyhow, I am sure he will write "Fifteen minutes of time *killed* deader than a door nail, and not a thing to show for it." He may write something more, but that is his affair, and not mine. To be a murderer of good time that has been *bought* and *paid* for is a bad enough record for any one to have to face.

And please do not try to turn this thrust of mine aside by saying it is exceptional, and that not one teacher in a thousand does such work as this, for such is not the case. I cannot tell how sorry I am to be compelled to say this, but the truth ought to be told, and I have told the truth in what I have written above.

I grant that the case I have noted is a *very* bad one, and that there are few as bad; but the visitation of more than fifty different schools in the last month has satisfied me that there is very much less *teaching* done in our schools than is commonly supposed, and that there are *very* few teachers, take them as they go, who have the tact to teach each one of the pupils under their care, *just where they especially need teaching.*

For instance: I saw a class of about twenty pupils working in proportion, a few days ago, and when I gave them a little simple problem, in which it happened to be necessary, in one operation, to divide by 8, a majority of the class used *long division* in doing the work !

And this did not occur in a backwoods town, either,

and it was the principal of the school who was hearing the class!

And the teacher said nothing to all this. When asked about it, he said that he never noticed how the children did their work! Perhaps he is an exception, too. I hope he is. But there are a good many exceptions that I see, or else I am unfortunate in happening upon them.

Because, when I went into a high school, last week, I heard a class in Latin "reciting." That is what the "exercise" was called.

I sat before the class for ten minutes, and during all that time there were only two short sentences translated, and only *one* of these was well done.

Nearly every member of the class took a hand at the *other* sentence, but failed to get anything out of it; and all this time the teacher (?) sat at his desk. He was a man, and a regular college graduate. (I insist that I am not bitter; I only tell the truth, just as I saw it), but did he nothing but call on pupil after pupil to rise, blunder, and fail, and be marked low for the same; when the fact was that there was a tricky little place in the sentence, something that the pupils had never had before, and which they needed just a little bit of *teaching* about.

But this they did not get. They got low marks; and the sentence was left untranslated, with the injunction to the class to "look it up."

Again, I heard a spelling class, to which twenty-five *hard* words had been given (this was in an upper grade in a grammar room) to learn to spell at a single lesson. Among the words I remember liquefy, guarantee, kiln, encrysted, separate, and there were twenty more of just about "the same degree of hardness."

These words had been written on the board by the teacher the day before, and were pronounced to the pupils, who wrote them at the recitation I heard. I saw the result, and out of the thirty-three who wrote there were only five who made a perfect record, while the majority of the class missed from three to ten words.

But they were all marked, and the marks recorded!

As to those who missed words, there was no attempt made to teach these pupils how to make a success out of failure. Indeed, there was no *teaching* done at all, so far as I can see, anywhere along the whole line of the exercise. It was just another case of "Go read your book" and "look it up."

The exercises over, the teacher wrote another twenty-five words on the board, for the next day. That was all. There was nothing said about the words, none of their hard places noted and pointed out to the pupils — not a particle of *teaching* done.

And I could not help wishing that the teacher would *teach* a little. That he would say to the pupils, when he wrote "liquefy" on the board, "Now, the hard thing about this word is the "e" after "qu." If you are not careful you will write "ify" for "efy." Or, that he had called attention to the fact that it is a very easy thing to write "sepe" for "sepa," when writing "separate."

I believe if he had done that, or the like of that, for a few times — that is, if he had *taught* the pupils how to study words — how to look after, and pick out, and fix upon, the hard places in every word they were set to learn to spell — if he had done this, if he had put the grease where the squeak was, he wouldn't have had such a poor lot of spelling books as came to his desk the day I was there.

And the people who hire this man to teach their children to spell would have got a good deal nearer the worth of their money out of his work than they are now getting, if he had used some such method.

And it is *results* that we must get!

It will not do to blame the previous teacher and excuse ourselves by saying that if the pupils would study they could get their lessons. We must get results, anyhow. We must teach the children to read, and to write, and to spell, and what not, and to do these things *well*.

If they don't learn to do these readily *by themselves*, (as some children do, but as most of them do not), it is the business of the teacher to teach them how to do them.

That is what a teacher is for!

But, as I live, I find a great many teachers in the schools I visit who do not have this conception of what a teacher is for. They seem to think that it is a teacher's business to assign lessons; hear pupils say them over, if they can do so; mark them up or down, as the case may be; keep records and make up grades, and for all this to draw pay. As Hamlet says, "It is not, and it cannot come to good."

And now, please, do not accuse me of telling tales out of school, don't call me a tattle-tale, because I have written what I have written above. It is not a pleasant thing to do, to write thus. It has given me the "blues" so that I shall not get over them for a week, just to set all this down; but I feel that I must do it.

For, if something is not done along these lines, to make them somewhere near what they should be, the people who pay for all this are going to find it out one of these days, and have something to say about it that will be heard on the house-tops!

And this is a thing the teachers ought to look so sharply after that it should never happen.

We must make our schools so good that people cannot help sending their children to them, law or no law.

We must teach *all* the children so well that they shall all learn to the fullest extent of their several capabilities.

That is what success in the public school means, and nothing short of that is worthy of the name.

Meantime, let me call your attention to the fact that whatever is said in these pages is not *telling tales out of school.* It is only telling the truth *in school*, and that is surely legitimate.

In going about among the schools, I try not to be hypercritical, and not to expect too much ; and a great deal of the work that I see is most excellent ; some of it the very best. Indeed, every once in a while I run up against something that I have been accustomed to think of, and to talk about as impossible, and yet I find it done, and done well in spite of what I may have said or thought.

For instance, I have for years thought it impossible for one who could not sing to teach singing in school, and especially to teach it well. I have seen the thing tried a good many times, and the most dismal failure made of it. But less than a month ago I was in a primary school and saw some of the best teaching of singing that I ever witnessed, done by a teacher who can scarcely sing a note ! But she was a woman of resources, and she knew how to *teach.* She did something more than to tell the children to " Go read your book," or to " Look it up ! "

But what I see, day after day, impresses this thing upon me, namely, that there is a great amount of what must be truthfully called " sloppy " work now done in our public schools. And further, that there is too little genuine *teaching* done in these schools, and a vast deal too much hearing of recitations and of telling the pupils to " look that up."

I do not mean that pupils should be told everything

— that they should be " carried to the skies on flowery beds of ease," but I do mean that they should be *taught.* That is the word.

Beloved, can you *teach ?* If your pupils do not *know,* can you *teach* them so that they *will know ?* These are questions to think about.

Can you tell where the squeak is in each child's mental mill, as you attend to its running, day after day ; and have you the skill to put the grease of your teaching right where the squeak is, when once you have found it out ?

If you are possessed of these qualities, you are a teacher blessed of God ; but if you are working in a school room without them, give up your place as soon as you can, and then, when you come to die, you can be reasonably happy in your mind.   But otherwise !   Well, you know.

HOUSE-CLEANING AND HISTORY.

We have been house-cleaning at our house for the last few days, and as I was just home from my winter's tour, and was taking a few days off, with nothing to do but "loaf and invite my soul," somehow or other, almost before I knew it, I found myself greatly interested in this annual festivity, which I had often heard of by the hearing of the ear but had never before really been part and parcel of, as it were.

As I stood off and watched the performance in detail, during the first few days of the epidemic, I gradually fell into the spirit of the occasion, and finally volunteered to "make a hand" at the business for a day, just for the sake of the new experience, sensation or what you will.   And I got all I bargained for, *and something left over.*

· And it is this something left over that I am going to write about, in what follows.

The first thing the mistress of the house put me at, (for it is she who always presides on these gala occasions) was the clearing out and regulating of a large store-room that was crammed full of a promiscuous lot of ancient *lares et penates* that once had had a more honorable place among our household goods and gods. I had never looked into the collection before, and had no idea that we possessed such a thesaurus of back-number truck, such a store of antiquities — or, rather, such a heap of rubbish!

To begin with, I was told to take all this stuff out of the room, then clean it and dust it, and return it to its proper place, and " regulate " it as I put it back.

It was not regulated when the job was turned over to me.

I started in on the work, got the articles all out, and the room " empty, swept, and garnished." I even began to clean and furbish up the relics that I had removed, and made ready to return them and regulate them.

But it was hard work, so I sat down to rest for a minute, and as I rested, I reflected.

It is a good thing to sit down and rest once in awhile, and while one rests to reflect.

As I reflected, these ideas came to me:

What is the use of keeping this miscellaneous lot of crippled and out-of-date stuff any longer?

What is it good for, anyway?

Have we ever made any use of it during the quarter of a century that it has been accumulating, since we began to keep house?

Why should that dozen or so of three-legged or broken-backed chairs ever again be cleaned, dusted, returned, and regulated?

Why longer keep that old cord bedstead, the ends of whose side pieces used to screw into the tall posts with right-and-left-hand threads, but which same threads are now mostly splintered off, till they cannot be screwed either way, but will slip out of their old sockets and let the whole thing fall to pieces, even if one should ever try to set it up?

And these old cracked jars, and broken-nosed pitchers, and battered stove-pipes, and empty picture frames with the gilt peeled off, and the whale-oil lamps, and rolls of wall-paper left over from various paperings of the house through the years — rolls laid aside because we thought we *might* need them to patch sometime, but which never matched when we tried to use them, because the paper on the walls was so faded.

(Who was it that said, long ago, " No man putteth a piece of new cloth on an old garment?"

And the worn out clothes wringer, and the broken jig-saw frame, and the bag full of old dress patterns, and ruptured fish-nets, and umbrellas with fractured ribs and punctured covers, and so on to the end of the heap,— *What is the use*, I thought, of cleaning and dusting and returning and regulating all this rubbish heap?

So I called the mistress of the house and told her what I had been thinking about, and we held a council, right then and there, with my thought as the basis of consideration.

This council lasted just two minutes, at the end of which time I started a bonfire in the back yard, and into that bonfire went every one of those useless, antiquated, worn-out, and broken-down things, that once had a name and a useful place in our lives, but which had had their day, and were fit now only for cremation.

It was a big fire, and a hot one; and as I stood and watched it, it really seemed to me that those ancient and fragmentary wrecks actually smiled out of the flames, while the crackle that came to my ears from the blaze was like jolly laughter, as if even these inanimate things realized that their end had finally come and they were glad of it.

There is such a thing as living too long in this world!

And then I cleaned and dusted and carried back and regulated what few *live* and still useful things were left over of the once monstrous pile. They filled one small corner of the room, and on the wide, ample space of the clean floor that was left after they were all in place, wife and I danced a horn-pipe in honor of the great deliverance that we had experienced, and because we had time to dance instead of cleaning and dusting and lugging back and regulating those cart-loads of rubbish.

Besides this, we were able to dance from the fact that we were not worn out by the doing of a quantity of useless, yes, worse than useless work, handling a lot of dead waste truck that was of no use to us or anybody else.

So we had a good time instead of being "dead tired," and there is space in the store-room that it is a pleasure to behold. We can use that space too, for things that we need every day, in our practice.

Well, a few days after this episode, I dropped into a school-room. Whatever comes or goes, I keep dropping into school-rooms; somehow they have a wonderful fascination for me.

There was a class in history reciting —

I wonder if I need go any further with this paper, or whether it would not be better to let each one of you "sing it yourself," from here out?   But I will tell the story.

"Mary may begin the lesson," said the teacher of the history class.

So Mary rose and said: "Surmising that an expedition, conducted by Clinton, which had been previously sent from Boston, was destined to attack New York, Washington sent Gen. Charles Lee to protect that city. It happened that on the very day of Lee's arrival there, Clinton arrived off Sandy Hook.   Thus foiled in his attempt against New York, Clinton sailed to the South, and was joined by Sir Peter Parker and Lord Cornwallis, with a fleet and troops from England, when the whole force proceeded against Charleston."

"That will do, Mary," said the teacher, "George may go on."

And George stood up and said: "The people of Charleston had made preparations against attack, by erecting a fort of palmetto-wood on Sullivan's Island, which commanded the channel leading to the town. This was garrisoned by five hundred men, under Col. Moultrie. On the morning of the twenty-eighth of June, the fleet approached Sullivan's Island; but, after a conflict of nine hours, during which Clinton was defeated in his attempt to reach the Island, the ships, much shattered, drew off, and afterwards sailed to the North."

And so it went on for twenty minutes; the pupils, one after another, standing and repeating from memory, the details of a fight that took place more than a hundred years ago!

The children had what would be called good lessons; that is, they had memorized some three or four pages of brevier type, and could say it off glibly; but I wondered if, when they sat down to rest and reflect, they did not think to themselves: What is the *use* of this old rubbish heap of carnage that we have labored so hard to carry out, and clean and dust and carry back and regulate?

What do you think the *use* of it is, beloved?

Or do you think about it at all?

Or do you do as was done with the stuff in our old lumber-room for years — just carry out, and clean, and dust, and carry back, and regulate, year after year, and never sit down to rest and reflect about it at all?

And when the class was excused, I said to the teacher: "May I look at that book for a little while?"

She said I might, so I took the history from which the class had been reciting, and sat down to it with my note book for half an hour, and read, and noted, and reflected.

Here are some of the things I noted.

In the first place, at least three-fourths of the book is taken up with detailed accounts of battles, fights, skirmishes, massacres, slaughters, and the like! Do you doubt that? Pick up the first school history you come to, and spend a half hour with it, as I did with this one, and make notes, as I did; see what you find, and then reflect.

Here are the printed questions from the foot of one of the pages the children recited from.

What can you say about the expedition against New York?

What was done by Clinton?

What was done by Clinton and Parker?

How were the people of Charleston prepared?

Give an account of the battle fought there?

Where, meanwhile, were the British concentrating a large force?

What troops joined Howe there?

What is said of the Hessians?

What move did Howe make from Staten Island?

Give an account of the battle there?

Give an account of the battle of White Plains?

To what objects did Howe next turn his attention?

And so on. It runs on like this for pages and pages. I would give more of it to prove my point, were it not that these pages are too devoted to "live matter" to have room for any more of this rubbish from an old lumber pile.

And if *this* is so, if there is no room on six-cents-a-pound paper for such things, how about the minds of your children having room for the like?

Just sit down and rest and reflect on that for awhile.

But let me "summarize" for a little, even if I may not proceed at length. School histories summarize a great deal. The one I made notes from (and it is as good as any — they are all substantially alike) summarizes to the extent of twenty-one pages, and the author then makes the remark:

"If these summaries are memorized they will do much towards enabling the pupil to retain, in compact form, the matter that is treated in a more extended manner in the body of the book." *Yea, verily!*

These twenty-one pages of summaries in this book, contain 655 dates, with memoranda attached.

There are also thirteen pages of "Review Questions."

There are 541 of these review questions, 420 of which are about battles, fighting, massacres, and the like.

In addition to this, the book contains 239 subjects for "Topical Review," the most of which subjects have for a hub, around which all else revolves, some battle, fight, massacre, general, colonel, captain or victim of some sort. I did not have time to count the details of this part of the book, for it came recess time before I got through, and I preferred to go and see the children play, rather than spend any more time numbering the dead!

Well, what do you think about it, when you come to sit down and reflect?

How would a bonfire do under the circumstances?

Don't you think that several of those 655 dates (I counted them every one! Don't stand up and tell me that I am "fighting a man of straw," and that "it is no such thing." I hear the like of that every now and then; but whatever I may have done or said heretofore, that is off or on, I am solid on this score; and if you are not satisfied with my count, you can make your own tally sheet out of any U. S. school history that you can find) — I say, don't you think there are several of those 655 dates that could be relegated to a bonfire and cremated, body and boots *so far as the school children's memories are concerned,* and this with profit to everybody?

Of course, it is all right and proper to have these dates and things set down in *books* so that we can get at them and *refer* to them if we ever have the occasion to; but to make the children carry them out and clean them, and dust them, and cart them back, and regulate them — is not the great bulk of all this labor in vain?

And heaven knows there is enough *live* work to be done in this world, not to waste time on labor in vain. In a word, "life is too short" to warrant such a useless, not to say senseless, amount of labor upon that which has had its day, lived, died, and ought to be buried.

It was Jesus who said, "Let the dead bury their dead." And, anyhow, this thing is sure, that dead things ought to be buried or burned. I like burning myself.

So what about making a bonfire for the benefit of the history class, when you clear out your course of study, the next time you undertake that job!

When you get into that lumber-room, your course of study, and make ready to carry things out of it, and clean them, and dust them, and cart them back, and regulate

14

them, as you have to do, more or less, every season; when
you get tired, just sit down and rest and reflect; and then,
if you do not make a bonfire out of some of the old cord
bed-steads and empty picture frames and flameless lamps
and noseless pitchers and cracked jars that you find
there, why, then well, you may say the rest.

And as for *ancient* history, I think a good share of
that could be bonfired. Kings, Emperors, Popes, Doges,
Consuls, Priests, Shahs, Pharoahs, and all their quarrels
and squabblings, with the times and seasons of the same
—what a fine blaze they would make, and it is the only
fine thing they could make, as I count it.

The Sunday after all this took place, I went to
church — but no, I must draw the line there. These
pages are not for theological criticism. But if they were!

Some day, when I get grown up, I am going to write
a book on "The use of a bon-fire in this world, all along
the line."

Meantime, if you get impatient for that far day to
arrive, you can work the scheme out for yourself. It will
give you a great deal of pleasure to do this; and if you
know how, you can dance and give thanks on the clear
spaces you will make in this mundane sphere, if you will
only practice what you preach in your volume, "The true
relation that exists between a rubbish pile and a bon-fire."

But whatever you do, or do not do, in a general way,
please do not forget your history class. If ever a big, hot
bonfire was needed, it is right there, in the average history
class of a common school.

Will you not pile out a few things from that lumber
room, and see to it that they never get back to torture
and muddle the heads of your children again? I believe
you will; and if you do, what I had left over from my
house-cleaning this spring will have been to some purpose.

GEOGRAPHY AND MUSIC.

I wonder if I can be pardoned if I strike one more blow on the head of the nail that I have been hammering at for a good while now, namely, this giving the children wisdom and knowledge in wholesale quantities, so to speak.

I would not mention it again, only I see so much of it as I go about, that I *know* it is the worst fault, the most generally disseminated failing, in the schools of this country to-day.

I see it everywhere I go — the children crammed with great blocks and wads of alleged learning, hunks and balls of science or language that stick in their intellectual throats till they are well nigh mentally. strangled.

Witness the instance of the teacher in natural philosophy that I saw before his class a couple of weeks ago, who disposed of the steam engine, its construction and working, in *two* lessons; and of the dynamos, ditto, in a single recitation of half an hour, and all, as set down in the book !

And yet, right across the street there was a large electric plant, with magnificent steam engine and dynamos; but not a foot did either pupils or teacher set within that building, and not an eye among them all was opened to look into the wonderful workings that were going on within ear-shot of them all !

Why, right within sight and hearing of those boys and girls there was interesting and profitable work enough, in studying the engine and dynamo, to have kept them busy for a month ; and yet the whole subject was disposed of in three bookish lessons — abstractions that those young people will hold in memory till they can get examination marks on them, and then forget forever.

I wish I could truly say that this case was exceptional, but it was not. I see its like in the majority of the schools I visit. That is the truth I am pained beyond measure to confess.

Indeed, as I look over, in retrospect, the couple of hundred teachers that I have seen at work in their class-rooms in the past three months, the thing that rises up and appalls me is the very small amount of *teaching*, *real* teaching, that I have seen done.

These teachers *hear recitations*, they test the children to see if they have *memorized* this, that, or the other, and, *in the great majority of cases*, that comprises the bulk of the work done in the school-room.

Do *you* teach, or do you hear recitations ? Just ask yourself that question when you say your prayers to-night, and then be thankful or pray for forgiveness, according to the answer you get to your question !

I heard a sixth-grade class in geography the other day that was exceedingly typical of most of the work that is being done in that branch of study wherever I go.

And, by the way, what is the matter with geography in our schools just now. Somehow, to use the vernacular, this study seems to have got a black eye, all along the line.

Up in Chicago, a few days ago, the county superintendent of that great county stated, in the presence of his teachers there assembled, that, as a pupil, he had studied two geographies. One he remembered was Peter Parley's, and the other he was not sure of, but he rather *thought* it was Mitchell's !

Of the first book, he said that all he could call to mind was the two lines:

> "The earth is round and like a ball
> Seems swinging in the air."

He could not finish the verse, but even so, he said that he remembered more of Peter Parley than he did of the other book, whatever that might have been!

And if you had heard the applause that followed this frank statement of Mr. Bright's, as the teachers who were evidently greatly in sympathy with him in his open confession, clapped their hands, I think you would have realized what those same teachers actually think of geography as it is regularly taught in our schools, as a means of developing the mind!

There is a wonderful significance in such a little scene as the foregoing, when one comes to get into the real meaning of it.

But to this class: The lesson was on Florida, and the teacher stood at her desk *with her finger on the questions*, as she read them, one by one.

Fact!

I see the like frequently, especially in the geography class.

Teacher — "George, what is the shape of Florida?"

George (who is a boy of twelve, a sort of bullet-headed boy) — "It's round!"

Teacher — "Round, George? Think again!"

George — "Well, it's kinder funny lookin'!"

Teacher — "What do you mean by that, George? Be careful now!"

George — "Well, it's kinder round on the bottom, anyhow!"

Teacher — "That will do, George! Mary, what natural division of land is Florida?"

Mary "I don't know what you mean."

Teacher (evidently trying to teach) —"Why, Mary, we have natural relations and natural conditions; now, what should you think a natural division of land would be?"

(I quote verbatim from notes made on the spot!)

But Mary couldn't make it out.

Isn't this too bad? And yet this teacher had taught six years, and was getting fifty dollars a month!

I asked the superintendent about her, and he said he knew very well what a poor, weak teacher she was; "but," he added, "what can I do? She is a relative of two members of the board, who insist that she shall stay where she is, and it is sure death to me in my position if I try to put her out!"

He added, "I came within one of getting myself dropped out two years ago, when I stood up and attempted to get rid of a couple of weak teachers that I had then on my hands. They both happened to belong to the same church; and, to make matters worse, it wasn't the church that I attended, and so the cry was raised that I was against them because they were not religiously of my faith!"

"Well," he said, "I did get them out, but it wouldn't be safe for me to make another similar move for a year or two yet, or I shall be out myself."

And what can one say to such an argument as that? For my part, I am dumb. Nevertheless, I think it best to set the record of this fact down in these chronicles, for us to think about, and see what we had better do about the likes, as they come up now and then.

And they will come up!

But there is another side to it all, and, thank God, it it is the biggest and brightest side, too. And this great big bright side is the noble personality of the great bulk of the teachers I meet. They are good men and good women, the great mass of them; and while many of them teach books very poorly, still they are such "good fellows," men and women both, that the children get a great deal out of them in spite of everything.

That is the consolation I get in spite of the many discouraging things I see. It shows up at recesses and noons, and when the children meet their teachers just as "folks," and not as "Masters" and "Ma'ams."

And the system that brings children and men and women together thus, even though it has its faults, is on the right track, and is bound to come to good. Though we ought to *teach* more and better.

And what are we going to do about geography? Poor old geography!

If any one has a word of suggestion, speak up. As they used to say at prayer meeting, "there is an opening for prayer or remarks." Have *you* anything to say? Or, better, is *your* teaching of geography worth the time and trouble you and your pupils are giving it? If not, what are you going to do about it?

I visited a school in Wisconsin, last week, and while going the rounds, from room to room, I chanced upon the music-teacher of the school, a woman who was enthusiastic in her work, and who got most excellent results from her endeavors.

This teacher went from room to room, teaching music in all grades, from the lowest to the highest; and I was so much interested in what she was doing that I followed her from class to class, as she went about the building.

And the thing that impressed me, in nearly all her classes, was the fact that almost every child in every class

sang, and that they did so with reasonable accuracy, so
that the general effect was exceedingly pleasing.

I asked her about this as we walked down the hall
between the acts, questioning her as to the possibility of
making a singer out of each and every child that came to
school, and her answer was so sensible that it is a pleasure
to me to quote it, as nearly as I can remember it. She
said :

"Well, I'll tell you ; of course there are singers and
singers, and I simply try to do the best I can with what I
have to work with. But five years of experience has
taught me this : if I can get hold of a child young enough,
I can do *something* for him or her in the line of music.

"Not all of them, though, for once in a while I get hold
of a pupil that simply cannot learn to sing. But the great
bulk of them can do something at it, and many of them a
great deal.

"And in the last year or two I have stumbled upon a
way of handling my 'monotones'—that is what I call the
pupils who, when they first try to sing, do so all on one
pitch of voice—that has brought the most excellent results. I really don't know that the game is worth the
candle," she added, "but *if* it is worth while to try to
make all the children sing *some*, I have found a way that
does it fairly well.

"And this is what I do, and how my present method
differs from the plan I used for years.

"When I began my work, years ago, if I got hold of
a 'monotone' I would take such a pupil off by himself
and work with him alone, for hours, sometimes. And
while I labored *very* hard on such boys and girls, I never
got very much out of it.

"But now I do the very reverse of this. When I find
such a case, I seat the pupil where he will be surrounded,

on all sides, by children who naturally sing well. If you will pardon the expression, *I just soak him in music,* and hold him under, till, after a while, some of it begins to penetrate into him !

"And if I can get hold of such children young enough — can take them just as soon as they enter school, and at once begin to work them on this plan, I can, in the great majority of originally unpromising cases, get fair results ; that is, I can succeed in getting them so that they can sing *some* — at least they can sing when other people are singing with them, and sometimes some of them get so that they can sing fairly well by themselves.

"Though, as I have already said," she added, "I don't know that the outcome pays for all the labor it costs, both to the pupil and the teacher ; but still, if all the children must be taught to sing, I have found this method much the most satisfactory that I have ever tried."

And I wonder if there are not other cases where pupils who are "born short" in one line or another could be "soaked" in an environment of "longs" on their particular failing, and so, by a process of the most pronounced induction, be compelled to take on at least a semblance of what the regular thing demands that they shall be possessed of ?

It may be a pretty thin sort of coating that such pupils take on, but when a board, or a principal, or a curriculum, insists that these things shall be done, somehow, the soaking process seems to offer better chances of output than anything I have seen for a long time.

TWO AFTER-DINNER SPEECHES.

I took a walk into Chicago a few days ago went up to eat, drink, and be merry, with the Normal Club of the "Windy City."

And I found the town worthy of just that name, and fully sustaining all the reputation it has ever had for blow and bluster, to say nothing of bluff. A gale was coming in from the northeast, that threatened to take the lake up bodily and set it down, *en masse*, on Illinois soil. But that inland sea " kicked," as it were, at thus being routed out of its bed; and the result was that there were troublesome times on the surface of that generally civil piece of water. A score or more of vessels were driven ashore, and some twenty-five or thirty sailors were drowned.

We stood and saw the men go down some of them were only a little ways from the shore — down into the pitiless depths that swallowed them as if they were blocks of stone rather than men with human souls in their bodies.

As I stood with the crowd of several thousands of my fellow-men, and looked at the spectacle, I could but wonder at the calmness with which we saw those brave fellows, out there, go down into the Valley of the Shadow of Death!

There was very little said in all the vast crowd along the shore. The life-saving crew was at work, doing its best, which amounted to nothing at all; and we all stood there and looked on.

A ship would come driving in, dragging her anchor, strike the ground, and then go to pieces. The crew clung to the rigging, as best they could; but when the ship struck and the break-up came, everything went, and the men along with the rest.

And we stood there and looked at it all, and said nothing, did nothing.

What could we say? What could we do?

But the sight stayed with me for a long, long time. Indeed, I can see it all now when I shut my eyes.

And it almost gave me the blues. Indeed, if I could not look at it "in large," I think it would drive me frantic. But I am learning to believe that even wrecks at sea are provided for.

Did you ever think they were *not* provided for?

Do you think it is possible that there can be anything in this world that is *not* provided for, when *anything* is provided for?

These are things to think about.

Well, after I had looked as long as daylight lasted, I went down to the Hyde Park Hotel, where the Normal Club was to have its re-union and banquet. And down there one would never have dreamed that the lake was in a fury, and that men were dying by the score, within a few blocks of where we sat, all in our good clothes, and smiled at each other, and said wise things as we smiled.

There are so many things going on at once in this world that it is often confusing to keep track of them all, and to harmonize them, and account for them as all coming from the same source!

But I am persuaded that all things do come from *one* and the same source.

Did you think that *some* things in this world came from other than *one* source?

Did you ever try to think of some things in this world coming from other than *one* source?

What do *you* know of that comes so? Take a pencil and write down the name of the thing that *you* think comes from other than *one* source in this world!

When you get the name written down, look at it a long time, and think what source it does come from, if not from the *one* source of all things!

But at the banquet we had a most delightful time. There was no doubt about the source from which it came ·it, and all that went with it. Question as we might about the source of shipwrecks, the source of the joy and happiness that were everywhere present at that banquet-table was no mystery.

It is such a comfort to be sure of some things!

After the eating was over, the speaking of the occasion came on, and of all that was said on that occasion, there were two speeches, or talks, made then and there, that I want to make a record of.

The first was made by a noted professor of a noted university. I haven't his words in black and white before me, but I think they are pretty well stamped upon my memory, and I will try to report them, just as nearly as possible as he spoke them. Substantially, he said:

" I am very glad to speak of university work, and of the relation that should exist between the training in the public schools, and the work which is subsequently to be done in college.

"And I want to say that more and more the public schools should keep college work in mind as they arrange their courses of study and train their pupils.

" We in the college can only do our work well as you in the public schools do your work well, *and as that work is done with special reference to the college work which we have to undertake.*

"And so I am glad to see that the report of the Com-

mittee of Ten, on common-school *curricula*, has great re-
gard for the college-work which is to follow the common-
school work; and I am specially thankful for the work
that a western college president has done in the line of
getting more college-trend work into the common-school
courses of study," etc.

As I have said, these are not the exact words of the
speech, but they will serve to convey, fairly, I think, the
idea that the speaker had in mind and gave utterance to.

Well, when this speech was ended, some one called
on Miss Dryer; and before I try to tell what she said, I
ought to say a word about the lady herself.

Emeline Dryer was born some years ago, so long ago
that I studied grammar under her a quarter of a century
previous to the date of this writing. I have heard it
stated, on good authority, that she was born with her eyes
open; but be that as it may, she has always had a way of
seeing what there was to be seen, ever since I knew her,
and that is a good while.

She taught in the Illinois State Normal School for a
number of years, but about twenty-five years ago she
gave up her position there, and went to Chicago, where
she entered upon a line (I will not call it a " career;" the
lady is not a career sort of a woman) of special mission-
ary and charitable work. She has never said much about
it, for she is not much given to talk; but only God knows
what she has *done*.

So Miss Dryer, who came to the club meeting for
old times' sake, was asked to say something, and here is
about what *she* said (I again quote from memory):

" I am glad to see you all here, eating and drinking,
and enjoying yourselves. But it is not *you* that I am
anxious about as I stand here and talk to you.

"When I left the Normal School, I stepped down into what was to me an under world, a place full of people and conditions that I had never had any, not the slightest, conception of, till I got down into it and began to look around.

"And I want to say to you, good folks, here to-night, that it is not you whom I am concerned about, nor the higher education of which you have been talking — those things do not worry me in the least; but I am anxious about the relations that exist between you and your likes, and the thousands, and thousands, and thousands, and thousands, and thousands, and thousands, and thousands of children who, if they could see you sitting at this table and could hear what you are saying, would have no conception whatever of what it is all about; children by the cityfull, who know nothing about, and care nothing about a higher education, and who never *can* know or care about it, owing to the limitations and peculiarities of their natures; children who were never born to partake of a higher education, and for whom such education is a closed book and must always remain so; and yet children who will grow up into men and women who can annihilate you and all the ranks of societies that talk about, and have to do with, a higher education and what goes with it — *it is these children and the relation that the common schools hold toward them that I am anxious about.*

"These children can be educated, *but not on the line of a higher education, as that term is now interpreted!* The question is, *what are the common schools doing to educate them along the lines on which it is possible for them to become educated?* It is only along such lines that they can ever be trained to become valuable members of society; *and if they are* NOT *trained along these lines, they will become a plague in the body politic that will one day bring ruin to this noble land!* And what I am anxious about, and want *you*

to be anxious about, so far as the *public schools* are concerned is, *not* the higher education of a *few* who can go
to college, but *an* education for the *great hordes of the children* who never *can* go to college, and to whom it would
do no good, even if they could go to college! *Just think
that over when you get home!*"

That is about what she said, and then she sat down,
and a great hush, almost the silence of awe, fell on the
company as she took her seat.

I have said that these two speeches made a great impression on me, and they did!

And I would to God that they might make an impression upon you who read these lines, for they contain
the gist of the whole matter, so far as the public schools
are concerned, in this day and age.

Who hath ears to hear, let him hear.

Democracry is the watchword of these years and
democracy means all the people! And the democracy of
democracies *should be* the public schools.

The fathers of these schools honestly hoped, expected, and tried to make them true democracies, but they
did not succeed in their undertaking. The schools they
established, while they are nominally *for* all the children
of all the people, as a matter of fact meet the needs of
only a *small percentage* of these children.

*The great bulk of the children of the common people, in
this country, go to the common schools for only a very small
portion of their years of school age.* The reason they do not
go longer is, that *the schools are not suited to their needs!*

Can we make schools such as are suited to their
needs, and will we do it? That is the question that the
people of this land have got to answer.

If we do not, or cannot answer this question, and
that in the near future, the idea of popular education —

an idea which has been the corner-stone of our national faith and hope for nearly a century,—will soon come to be regarded as a delusive dream, the vagary of a well-meaning set of men, but not practical, as a matter of fact.

And when such belief takes hold of any considerable number of the people of these states, look out!

Walking abroad, as I have been doing for years, with an eye which I have tried to make single to the best interests of *all* the children of *all* the people; and having personally visited and inspected hundreds, not to say thousands, of our common schools in nearly every state in this Union, I find myself impressed, as I write these last words of the record of my wanderings, with the great idea that Miss Dryer so simply, yet forcibly, expressed in her after-dinner talk, namely, that *the public schools must educate all the children of all the people.*

They are not doing this now; and it is with the hope of helping *you* to realize this fact, and to stimulate *you* to do something to better the situation, and help on the cause of making these schools what they ought to be, that I have said what I have said in these pages, and herewith send my words to you, greeting:

Truly the Master said: "Say not to yourselves there are yet four months, and then cometh the harvest. But I say unto you, lift up your eyes to the fields, for behold they are already *white* for the harvest." And if the grain is not gathered it will spoil! Will *you* "make a hand" in this Public School Harvest Field?

www.ingramcontent.com/pod-product-compliance
Lightning Source LLC
Chambersburg PA
CBHW030128030726
47498CB00007B/2598